SULPHIDE GULCH

LIFE ON THE ALASKA FRONTIER

G.E. SHERMAN

Sulphide Gulch

ISBN-13: 978-1734464375

This work is historical fiction. Some of the incidents described herein may not exactly align with actual events of the period. All the characters in this book are fictional.

FLEETING EDGE PRESS, 2021

To Uncle Jack.

"The lack of money is the root of all evil."
Mark Twain

"Money has never made man happy, nor will
it, there is nothing in its nature to pro-
duce happiness. The more of it one has
the more one wants."
Benjamin Franklin

"It is not the man who has too little, but the
man who craves more, that is poor."
Seneca

"For the love of money is the root of all evil"
1 Timothy 6:10

Books in the
Life on the Alaska Frontier **series**

CONTENTS

The Trail to the Fortymile

0 10 20 30 40 50 60 70 80 miles

Chicken
Kechumstuk
Tanacross
Mentasta Pass
Indian Pass
Slana
Chistochina
Gulkana
Tazlina
Copper Center
Tonsina
Kimball Pass
Ernestine
Tiekel
Ptarmigan Drop
Valdez
Wortmanns

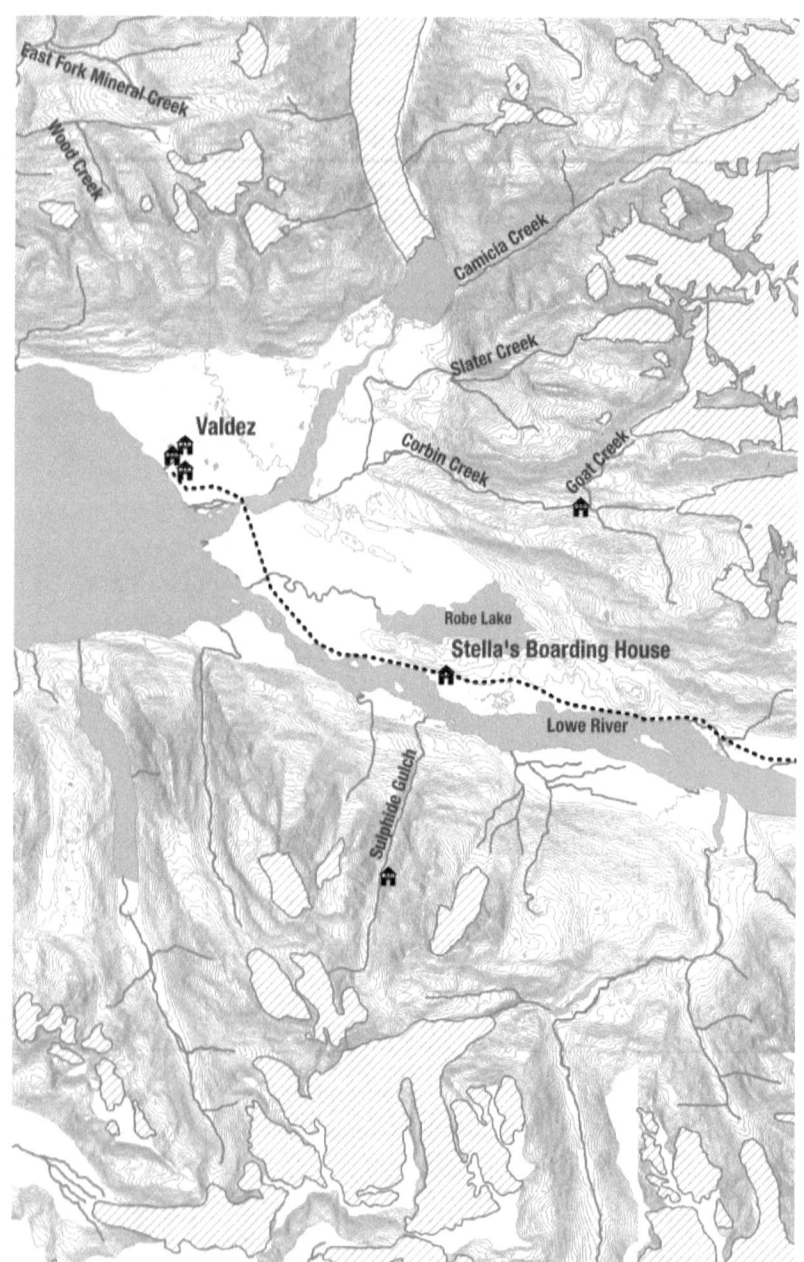

PROLOGUE

He sat on the edge of the Seattle steamship dock, his feet dangling over the shimmering blue water of Elliot Bay. The smell of the sea air was refreshing, despite the constant clamoring of the gulls that sailed back and forth, looking for a quick meal. Among the steamships was that stalwart of gold rush travelers, the *Northwestern*, currently tied up but readying for departure to Valdez and points in between. Thick black smoke from her coal-fired boilers filled the air—the distinct, biting odor an affront to the nostrils of everyone nearby.

He checked his aging pocket watch, a family heirloom of sorts—almost 9 a.m. *Nearly two years it's taken, but the time has come,* he thought as he stood and looked down the dock. *He better get here soon—the ship leaves in an hour.*

The gulls continued to circle the bright blue sky. He watched, wondering what it was like to fly—to be free and soar above the mundane, dirty world that comprised his existence. Poverty was his constant companion, yet he worked hard to clean himself up—to be something he wasn't. Years of menial labor were expended just to scrape together the fare to Alaska. It would have been easier to afford one ticket, but he needed two—needed help to succeed.

He pulled the wrinkled paper from his vest pocket and unfolded it—reading for the hundredth time. There it was—the chance, the opportunity to climb out of the pit he was in if only he could find it. The letter contained no clues, rather the mention of the prize—that it existed, that in the event of a tragedy, it could be obtained—by him.

He folded the letter and put it away, then looked at his watch again. *If he doesn't make this boat so help me...*

The ragged figure shuffled down the dock in no apparent hurry. He was shabbily dressed in an old wool suit that should have been relegated to the moths. His shoes were scuffed to the point of splitting and made an annoying squeak as he walked. "I made it," he yelled.

He looked at the unkempt fellow—Willy he called himself—a man you'd see in the shadowy neighborhoods of Seattle. He was badly in need of a haircut and a shave. His teeth were dark yellow, lips stained with tobacco, and he smelled like a stockyard. Good thing they weren't partners. He needed a simpleton, a dolt to help with the job, someone with no family connections and nothing to return to.

Willy approached and slapped him on the back. "Hey friend, I can't wait to get out of here."

"I'm not your friend. If you want to get paid, I want you to stay away from me, keep your hands off me, and do as your told."

"No need to get all huffy about it, friend."

He shook his head. *Too late to find someone else. This poor excuse for a human being will have to do.*

The *Northwestern* blew two short blasts of its horn, which caused the passengers milling on the dock to move toward the gangplank for boarding. The boilers belched a rolling cloud of black smoke as the deckhands made ready at the mooring bollards, waiting to release the lines holding the ship.

"We better go," said Willy.

He looked at him and motioned him onward.

"Not coming?"

"I told you. Stay away from me until we get to Valdez."

"You are a hard man for being only twenty-some years old."

He ignored the comment. "Get on board. We'll meet up in Valdez. Until then, you're on your own—you don't know me."

The man frowned, stared at him for a moment, then headed for the ship. He waited until his scruffy associate was on board, then made his way to the gangplank. He paused halfway up, one of the last to board, and took a look at his hometown, wondering if he would ever see it again.

I'll be back—if it all works out, he thought as he turned and boarded the *Northwestern*.

CHAPTER 1

The full moon illuminated the graveyard, neatly decorated with simple wooden crosses. The spring air was crisp, enough so that he could see his breath as he moved slowly among the markers. The ground was soaked from a recent rainstorm, the mud sticking to his boots as he walked carefully, hunched down for fear of being seen. Kneeling at each marker, he squinted in the dim light, finding the faded names hard to read. But, it was here—he was sure.

Though isolated, the graveyard could be seen from the little town of Chicken. He had to be careful—couldn't afford to be seen. The lantern in his pack wasn't an option—instead, he pulled the matches from his pocket and proceeded to examine each cross in turn, barely able to discern the names.

Apart from the others stood a single marker, leaning, seemingly isolated for a purpose. The grave was unkempt and overgrown, standing tall with grass and weeds. He flattened the grass around the cross and struck a match. In the flickering light, he found what he was looking for.

Removing the pack, he untied the short-handled shovel and plunged it deep into the soil. The loud echo was more than he expected. He ducked down low to the ground and waited—listening. Hearing nothing, he slowly

raised up and looked toward the town. A single flickering light shone from the window of one of the buildings.
He waited, watching, practically holding his breath. The
light remained, not moving.

He pulled out his pocket watch, struck a match, and
looked at the time. Nearly 2 a.m. There wasn't much
time to accomplish his task. He dug faster, quieter, hoping the grave was shallow.

Sweat rolled down his face, the hole now three feet
deep, yet not deep enough. He looked back toward the
town, hoping there were no early risers. Unfortunately,
it was an all-or-nothing proposition—he couldn't come
back another day and continue digging. He worked faster,
cringing each time the shovel struck a rock with a clang.
He wondered what time it was but didn't take the time to
look. He had to reach the coffin, he had to accomplish
his task, or there would be hell to pay.

His back was screaming. The blisters on his hands
threatened to break. *Should have worn gloves.* He looked
at his watch—after 3 a.m. and still not done. *Stay or go?*
He knew the consequences if he quit. Twenty yards from
the grave was a thick stand of aspen. If worse came to
worst, he could flee into the trees and make his escape.
Slightly reassured, he resumed digging. Three jabs of the
shovel later, he was rewarded with the dull thud of iron
on wood. He dug faster now, sliding the shovel along the
top of the coffin.

It quickly became apparent there was no way to un-
cover the entire thing before daylight. With about a third
of the coffin revealed, he switched tactics. It wasn't easy,
but using the shovel, he was able to pry loose one of the
rough-cut planks that made up the lid. Immediately the
unmistakable stench of decomposition assaulted his nostrils, causing him to gag. He covered his mouth, held his

breath, and tried to keep from losing his last meal. Recovering slightly, he continued prying and working the boards loose until he had partially exposed the corpse.

He gagged several more times, then struck a match. The lifeless eye sockets embedded in the withered flesh stared back at him as he brought the match close. Shocked at the sight, he dropped the match and it went out. *This is impossible. I'm running out of time.*

He was dirty, muddy, tired, and sick to his stomach. He removed more of the dirt from the coffin, but the hole kept sloughing in, making progress slow. He cursed and threw the shovel down, immediately regretting the thud as it hit the lid. *Get yourself together, man.*

He picked up the shovel and began prying again, wondering all the while what the penalty was for grave robbing. *Frontier justice, no doubt.* Standing in the hole at the head of the coffin, he grabbed a plank and pulled up with all his might. It sprung out of his hands, leaving him with several long slivers of rough-cut spruce. He cursed under his breath, then tried again. This time it cracked, allowing him to bend it up nearly vertical. He grabbed the next one, and with some effort, managed to do the same. Before long, the upper part of the coffin was open, the broken and splintered planks sticking up at odd angles, some leaning back against the edge of the hole.

A rooster crowed in the distance, causing a wave of panic to sweep over him. Time was running out. He struck a match, took a last look at the corpse, and got on with it.

† † †

CHAPTER 2

Thomas dumped the wheelbarrow into the sluice box and watched as the current swept the gravel away. The winter dump of paydirt from the underground drift mine had thawed enough on the surface to begin sluicing. It was slow going, but he had high hopes of a good season.

"Hey," said Sdzeè as she came down the trail, a steaming cup of coffee in her hand. "Time for a break."

Thomas clapped his hands together to shake off the dirt, then sat down on a nearby log. "Thanks. Married six months, and you're still spoiling me."

Sdzeè smiled and handed him the cup. "We work well together, Thomas Thornton."

"Come on. Don't you think you can dispense with using my last name by now?"

She laughed. "I do it to remind you who you are."

"I'm not that old—yet."

Sdzeè bent over the sluice box and removed the remaining rocks too heavy for the current to wash away. She fanned the water near the first riffle and leaned in closer, looking for the telltale sheen of gold.

Thomas looked at his wife, her long, jet-black hair draped over her shoulders. He'd known her for such a short time but couldn't imagine life without her. He took a swig of coffee. "See anything good?"

She reached in and plucked out a nugget about the size of a kidney bean. "How's this?" she said, holding out her hand.

"Excellent," said Thomas. "If that's any indication, we're going to have a good season."

Sdzeè nodded. "Too bad John and Stella aren't here to see."

The mention of their names brought back a flood of memories. The attempt by Samuel Pierce and his son to steal the claim—to murder all of them still burned in his mind. The image of John's daughter Emily lying there, mortally wounded, he and Stella trying to save her, still plagued him. Yet, thanks to Sdzeè, the plot was foiled.

"I think it was too painful for John to remain after Emily's death," he said finally.

"I hope they are doing well in Valdez," said Sdzeè as she continued browsing the sluice box.

"Me too. I need to go into town and send a telegram to see if everything is fine. We haven't heard from them in a while."

"Maybe they have sent word to us as well," said Sdzeè as she handed another small nugget to Thomas. She smiled broadly. "We are rich soon."

† † †

The telegraph office was locked when Thomas arrived. He looked around but found no sign of Wayne, the often late operator. He shrugged. *Might as well get a cup of coffee at the roadhouse.*

The street was still a bit muddy from the rain the day before but had dried considerably. Thomas dodged the puddles as he walked down the street, wondering why things seemed so quiet. Rounding the corner to the roadhouse, he noticed a group of people at the cemetery. Curious, he headed that way. Thomas hadn't heard of anyone dying, and the grapevine in the small community usually made sure news traveled fast.

"What's going on?" said Thomas as he edged his way into the small crowd gathered in the far corner of the cemetery.

"Looks like we've got a grave robber in town," said Wayne, pointing at the partially excavated hole.

Thomas moved closer. The wooden coffin made from rough-cut lumber wasn't completely exposed. The front had been pried open, partially revealing the corpse. The stench was nearly sickening, but more astonishing was the condition of the body.

"The clothes are gone," said another of the onlookers. "Who would dig up a grave just to take the clothes off a poor dead guy?

"You know who that is?" said Wayne, turning to Thomas.

Thomas nodded and took another look at the body. Indeed the clothes were gone, leaving a ghastly sight. He wasn't repulsed by the view but rather indignant—it was the body of Preston Van Sant. The man that caused John much grief, stealing his fortune, burning the home in Seattle to the ground, and making off with his wife. Worst of all was the attempt on John's life, an event vivid still in Thomas' memory—the day he took a life to save another. He held his breath and backed away from the hole.

"I'm surprised he isn't more rotten after all this time," said Wayne.

Thomas shrugged. "I guess being buried in the cold ground has something to do with it."

"You shot him, right?" said Wayne.

Thomas frowned. "I had to—he was about to shoot John in cold blood."

"Ah, right," said Wayne. "Bad business that was."

Bad indeed. It was beyond puzzling. Why would someone dig up Van Sant's grave after more than a year? It wasn't like there was anything of value to be found. Thomas looked around. "None of the other graves bothered?"

"No. Just this one."

Thomas shook his head, then turned to Wayne. "I need to send a telegram and see if any are waiting for me. You going back to the office anytime soon?"

"Yeah, I should be getting back. A couple of the fellas went to get shovels to bury the poor sod."

I wouldn't waste a handful of dirt on him, thought Thomas as he turned and headed back toward the telegraph office.

✝ ✝ ✝

"Don't see anything for you here," said Wayne as he shuffled through the small stack of messages on the counter. "I probably would've remembered getting something for you anyway."

Thomas nodded, took the blank pad, and began writing a message to John and Stella.

```
JOHN & STELLA PALMER
VALDEZ ALASKA

HOPE ALL IS WELL THERE. DOING
FINE HERE. WORK PROGRESSING
NICELY. SDZEÈ AND I WISH YOU
WERE HERE.

/S/ THOMAS THORNTON
CHICKEN ALASKA
```

Thomas put down the pencil, then paused, wondering if he should mention the odd event in the cemetery. John would certainly be interested, but perhaps it would dredge up memories he didn't need to deal with. *No, it can wait until another time.*

"Here you go," said Thomas, handing the message to Wayne. "How much?"

Wayne started to count the words in the message, then stopped. "Ah, heck. I'll send this one for free. I like old John."

"Well, thanks a lot. I appreciate it. I'll catch you next time."

Wayne nodded and sat down at the telegraph key. "I'll send it off right now."

Thomas reached the door and turned. "Thanks again. I'll check back for a reply in a day or two."

The key was chattering away as Thomas closed the door behind him. He looked toward the cemetery. The crowd had dispersed—only two figures remained, slowly shoveling dirt into the desecrated hole.

✝ ✝ ✝

Sdzeè was busy working on a pot of caribou stew when Thomas returned from town. The smell of *udzih* stew brought back fond memories for Thomas, how she had rescued him after his fall through the ice. He smiled at the thought of that first encounter in her cabin.

"I am making your favorite," she said, tapping the wooden spoon on the side of the pot.

"I see that. I hope there will be biscuits too."

"Don't push your luck, Thomas Thornton," she said, shaking the spoon at him, then smiling.

"I'll get some wood for the stove."

Thomas returned with the wood and dropped it into the box next to the big cast-iron stove. He looked around the cabin, thankful it was larger and better equipped than the one he and John lived in on Angel Creek. After combining their mining operations, they concentrated on Sdzeè's claim, making occasional visits to Angel Creek. When John and Stella left for Valdez, they made Sdzeè's cabin their permanent base of operations.

"Did you get a telegram?" asked Sdzeè.

"No, there was nothing for us, but I did send one to the Palmers. There was something odd going on in town though."

"Oh?"

Thomas told her about the digging in the cemetery and the odd fact that the clothes were missing from Van Sant's corpse.

"Van Sant? He is the one who caused so much trouble here—before we met."

"Yes, he was an angry, bitter man. Who knows the extent of his crimes."

"But it is very odd, the theft of clothes."

"I agree. I can't imagine anyone here doing that. I'll ask around tomorrow when I go to check for an answer from John. Maybe find out if there's someone new in town."

"Good idea," said Sdzeè. "Ready for stew?"

Thomas looked at her and smiled. "Where's the biscuits?"

✝ ✝ ✝

CHAPTER 3

John Palmer loaded the last box of food and supplies into the wagon and waved at the clerk still staring
at him through the window. Since returning to Valdez
nearly a year ago, the boarding house saw steady business but nothing exceptional. Most people headed over
the Valdez-Eagle trail for the goldfields in interior Alaska
stayed in town at the hotel before departing. There was
enough business to keep things at the house running and
provide a moderate living. Plus, they had a bit of money
in the bank, yet still, he worried. At the moment, the
boarding house was full, and Stella was antsy for resup-
ply to keep the tenants happily fed.

He jumped up onto the wagon seat, then changed his
mind. *Might as well check the telegraph office while I'm
here.* He had pretty much given up on ever recovering
the money Van Sant stole, leaving him penniless, yet his
private investigator in Seattle was still on the case. Little
could be done other than keeping an ear to the ground for
new tidbits of information. John held out a bit of hope
that someday he would get good news—that ultimately
his fortune would be recovered. There was no word from
the investigator in months, but that was to be expected if
there was no progress.

"Greetings, Mr. Palmer. What can we do for you today?" said the clerk as John entered the telegraph office.

"Just thought I'd check to see if there was anything for me since I'm in town."

"Ah, yes, I believe we got something for you yesterday—let me check."

The clerk shuffled through a stack of messages, found nothing, then reached for another pile and started going through it. "Here it is," he said, waving a slip of paper, then looking at it.

"Great," said John, holding a slim hope it was from Seattle.

"It's from Chicken," said the clerk as he handed it to him.

John read the message from Thomas. It was good to get brief word from him, yet it brought back a flash of pain at the mention of his daughter. He put the image out of his mind.

"Any reply?" asked the clerk.

John thought for a moment, then decided against it, wanting to ask Stella if she had news to include in a message. "I'll wait," he said as he headed for the door. "Maybe have something to send later this week."

"Very good, sir," said the clerk as John pulled the door shut behind him.

I hope we made the right decision returning to Valdez, he thought as he mounted up and turned the wagon toward home.

† † †

John unhitched the wagon and led the horse into the barn. He picked up the wooden crate of supplies and entered the back door of the boarding house, which led directly to the kitchen. Stella was there, working on her next culinary creation for the guests.

"You're back," she said. "Get everything?"

John placed the crate on the counter. "Everything ordered, ma'am."

Stella smiled and gave him a peck on the cheek. "Go anywhere else?"

"Just the telegraph office. Got a message from Thomas," he said, reaching into his pocket and handing it to her. "Sounds like things are going well."

Stella read the note, then handed it back to John. "Did you send a reply?"

"No, I thought I'd check with you to see if you wanted to add anything in particular."

"Not really. Just tell them we're busy here and miss them." Stella looked into his eyes for a moment. "No other good news then?"

John knew what she meant. They could survive without the money, but it would provide options, especially if the boarding house business began to trail off.

"No, nothing more. I'll go and send a reply tomorrow. Might send a message off to Seattle as well—just to check."

Thomas shuffled to the steam boiler to shut it down. It had been a long day of work on the mine. The shaft to the underground workings was covered and insulated to prevent thawing of the workings. Over the winter, he and Sdzeè had mined enough pay gravel to keep them busy all summer. Unfortunately, as they brought each load to the surface and added it to the pile, it froze in the subzero temperatures. Though spring had arrived, it was still early in the season, and the dump was largely frozen, except for a foot or so on the surface. Using the wood-fired boiler and steam points, they thawed enough material each day to run through the sluice. Soon spring would melt into summer, the sun would be high in the sky, the days would be eighteen hours long, and the temperatures would approach eighty degrees. In a month or so, the pile of paydirt would completely thaw. But for now, it was the same routine—fire up the boiler in the morning, thaw gravel, load gravel, dump it in the sluice, then repeat.

"Time for dinner soon," said Sdzeè. "We have worked too hard today."

"Let's keep it simple. I don't want you slaving away making a fancy dinner."

Sdzeè smiled. "None of my food is fancy."

"Let's just have breakfast for dinner. Eggs and bacon work for me."

Sdzeè nodded. "Can do," she said as they started up the trail to the cabin.

As they walked, Thomas couldn't get the scene at the cemetery out of his mind. Tomorrow he definitely needed to go to town and ask around. He wasn't sure what it meant, or if he should tell John.

† † †

CHAPTER 4

"Heading to town early?" said Stella as she set a plate of fried potatoes, bacon, and eggs on the table in front of John.

John looked up at her and smiled. "You spoil me. Or are you just serving me leftovers from the boarders?"

"You'll never know," she said, sitting down across from him with a cup of coffee.

"To answer your question, yes, I'm headed to the telegraph office."

"I thought so since you were up and eager. You sending one to Seattle as well?"

"I think so. We haven't heard from the private investigator in a while. It's worth checking in with him, but I don't expect much."

"Well, in any event, Thomas and Sdzeè will be happy to hear from us."

"Do you have anything else you want to tell them, apart from missing them?"

"Nothing in particular. Just give them my love."

"Will do," said John as he prepared to stuff a bite in his mouth.

"You don't have to shovel it in, mister," said Stella, then grinned at him.

"I've lost my genteel table manners after being away from Seattle for so long."

Stella shook her head and returned to the kitchen. "I've got to get prepared for breakfast. The boarders will be clamoring for coffee and food soon."

John finished up his breakfast and brought the plate to the kitchen. "I'll be back soon—don't plan on doing anything else in town other than send the telegrams."

Stella nodded and continued slicing potatoes and tossing them into the cast-iron skillet sizzling with lard.

"Don't spoil the boarders too much. We want them to leave eventually," he said as he grabbed his coat and hat off the hook by the back door.

Stella laughed. "Gotta keep them happy."

"Right. See you soon," said John, waving as the door slammed behind him.

It took him a few minutes to saddle the horse—no need for the wagon today. He double-checked the cinch, then swung up into the saddle and headed down the trail. The horse knew the way—he was free to daydream or smoke his pipe if he cared to.

He thought about life in Valdez, an existence that was boring at times. At the mine up north, there was always plenty to do—plenty to occupy your time. Here, he had little to do except bring in the winter wood and fix up things around the boarding house. With little to do, he found too much time to think—and to grieve over his loss. He lit the pipe and let the horse plod along. *Perhaps the private investigator will have good news*, he thought, despite his skepticism.

† † †

"When are you going to town?" asked Sdzeè as she plunged the shovel deep into the gravel pile.

"As soon as you finish moving that entire pile through the sluice," said Thomas.

"Very funny, Thomas Thornton."

Thomas laughed. "It's nearly lunchtime, and we've been at it for nearly six hours. Let's take a break, and I'll go. You want to come along?"

"No. I will stay here. You go. Maybe I will find a big nugget while you are gone."

"Just remember we share. Don't you dare hide any nuggets from me."

Sdzeè laughed. "You will never know."

"That's it. I'm leaving," said Thomas, faking disgust.

He took off his gloves, slapped them together, then tossed them in the wheelbarrow. He headed toward the cabin to fetch the horse.

"Don't be gone too long," said Sdzeè loudly.

Thomas didn't look back but waved, knowing he may be gone longer than she thought. The mystery of the grave robber was something he had to solve. Chicken was a small town, but it might take a while to find out if anyone knew anything—if someone saw something suspicious.

It was nearly five miles from Sdzeè's cabin to town. The trail followed the north bank of the Mosquito Fork for roughly three miles until it met the Valdez-Eagle trail. The first part of the trail was narrow, with the river on the right and a steep mountain slope on the left. It was rarely traveled, except to reach Sdzeè's mining claim. The horse was familiar with the route, but Thomas was still on edge—portions of the trail had sloughed, making a plunge into the river a real risk. *I really need to do some trail maintenance.*

As he rounded a sharp bend in the trail, the horse

flared her nostrils and balked. Thomas was about to kick her in the ribs, then noticed why—a cow moose with twin calves blocked the narrow trail, and she wasn't happy. The moose had her ears laid back, and the hair on her back stood on end. The chocolate brown twins were barely two weeks old and hung back from their mother, huddled behind her rear legs.

Thomas pulled back on the reins and the horse backed up, sending rocks tumbling into the river a mere three feet below them. There was nowhere to go—barely enough room to turn around, but that wasn't an option. He didn't want to turn his back on the angry mother. He backed the horse further and she stumbled, sending a slide of dirt and rocks into the water. The moose had her head down, just ten yards from him. Thomas shouted, but the cow only became more agitated. He knew full well that a cow moose with calves can be just as dangerous as a bear.

The horse was thoroughly spooked and struggled against the reins. Thomas patted her neck and spoke softly, all the while hoping the moose would back off—she didn't. He pulled the .44-40 carbine from the scabbard, ready in case it all went south. *Come on, mother, take the twins and leave. I don't want to shoot you.* Shooting her meant certain death for the calves—they would quickly become a meal for a bear or wolf.

With the horse steadied and backed up onto more stable ground, Thomas yelled again. "Go on! Git!"

The cow put her head down and charged forward as Thomas raised the carbine, finger on the trigger. She didn't stop, and he dared not wait a moment longer. As he squeezed the trigger, the cow stopped suddenly, her front legs jutted out, and she skidded to a stop in the soft dirt of the trail. Thomas jerked the carbine up as the shot went off, sending it over her head. The moose whipped around and ran past the twins, anxious to escape. The calves ran after her, their legs moving twice as fast, trying to keep up.

Thomas patted the horse to steady her, glad she was accustomed to the sound of gunfire. He lowered the carbine and took a deep breath, his pulse returning to normal. After several minutes, the moose moved out of sight, and he nudged the horse gently forward, the carbine laid across his lap just in case. He could see fifty yards or so down the trail, and she was nowhere in sight. Beyond that, the route took a couple more sharp bends before intersecting the Valdez-Eagle trail. *Best move slowly,* he thought, pretty sure the moose wouldn't risk another confrontation.

He rounded that last bend before the main trail, where the mountain slope became more gentle. On his left, he spotted the moose, now a hundred or more yards off the trail. He watched as they moved uphill through the grass and alders, then breathed a sigh of relief, shoved the carbine into the scabbard, and nudged the horse onward.

†　†　†

John finished the message to Thomas and handed it to the clerk.

"We'll get this out straight away," said the clerk.

"I've got one more to send," said John as he took the blank pad and started to write.

```
CHARLES JACKSON
JACKSON INVESTIGATIONS
SEATTLE, WASHINGTON

ANY WORD ON LOCATING STOLEN FUNDS?
PLEASE ADVISE AS SOON AS POSSIBLE.
```

```
JOHN PALMER
VALDEZ, ALASKA
```

The message was short and to the point. John wished there was something he could add to further the investigation, but Van Sant left no clues. Even his dying words were hostile, filled with hate, and of no use finding the money. John handed the message to the clerk and waited while he counted up the words.

"Still looking for that money, eh sir?"

John frowned, aggravated at the continual invasion of privacy required when communicating via telegraph. "What business—never mind. How much?"

The clerk rubbed his forehead for a moment, then finished marking up the receipt for the message. "Here," he said, handing it to John.

John pulled out his wallet, slapped the money on the counter, crossed his arms, and waited.

"Change, sir?"

"Yes, if you don't mind."

The clerk fumbled in the cash drawer and finally came up with the right amount. John slid the coins across the counter and into his hand.

"Must you read every single message?"

The clerk took a deep breath and stepped back from the counter. "Sorry, sir, but we have to count up the words, and then the operator must read it as it's sent.

"A necessary evil, I guess," said John, resigned to the fact that privacy was impossible. "Is it possible for you to deliver a message to Stella's boarding house if there is a reply?"

"We can do that," said the clerk. "Might take a day or two since we normally just have the stage driver do that on his way north. Not sure when the next scheduled trip is."

John rubbed his chin and stared at the counter. "Fine, do that, please."

The clerk saluted, and John turned, slamming the door a little too hard as he left the office. He immediately regretted it but decided not to return and apologize. It surprised him that he was aggravated over the whole affair, especially since it had been so long since the money disappeared. He was anxious for word, but it didn't make sense to travel to town every day to check. He took a deep breath. *Better settle down before I get home*, he thought as he untied the horse and mounted up. He kicked her a little too hard in the ribs, and she took off with a gallop, her hooves throwing clods of dirt into the air.

† † †

The man watched the rider gallop down the street until he was out of sight, then entered the telegraph office. It was small, with a counter and beyond that, a desk where the operator sat. A small window over the desk allowed a stream of light to filter into the cramped space. Behind the counter stood the clerk, shuffling stacks of paper.

"Can I help you?" said the clerk as he looked up.

"Yes, I'd like to send a message."

"Oh, very good," said the clerk as he handed the man a pad and pencil. "Just scribble it down there."

He picked up the pencil and started to write, then paused. "Say, who was that man that just left?"

"Why do you ask?" said the clerk, squinting.

"Well, I think I know him but can't place him."

"Ah, I see. That's John Palmer—he and his wife run the boarding house up the trail a bit."

"Oh, Palmer—right."

"Where do you know him from, if I might ask, sir?"

The man put the pencil down and looked squarely in the clerk's eyes. The clerk returned his gaze for a few seconds, then broke it off and looked down at the counter.

"Seattle. I think I've seen him in Seattle," said the man.

"Oh right, sir. He's from Seattle—came up nearly two years ago."

"He come in here often?"

"Fairly often. Just sent a couple of messages today—one to Seattle, as a matter of fact."

A thin smile spread across the man's face, then was quickly extinguished. He looked at the telegraph operator, busy copying Morse code and writing down the messages as they came in. The pile of incoming messages sat on the far side of the desk, just to the operator's right.

"Actually, can you check to see if anything has come for me from Seattle?"

"Sure, your name?"

"Lowe, Erik Lowe."

The clerk laughed.

"Something funny?"

"Oh, nothing, just that river that flows into the bay here is the Lowe River."

"Different Lowe. How about that message."

The clerk shuffled through the messages while Lowe waited for his opportunity, all the while eyeing the stack of sent messages just to the right.

"Nothing here," said the clerk.

"How about in that stack over there," he said, pointing to the operator's desk.

"Oh, I'll look," said the clerk as he turned away and began flipping through the slips of paper on the operator's desk.

Lowe leaned over the counter and looked at the message on top of the sent stack—the one Palmer had just sent. He scanned it, thankful it was short, then quietly slid it aside to read the second one. *Thornton...* Lowe tidied up the stack and leaned back from the counter.

The clerk turned back toward the counter. "Nope, sorry, Mr. Lowe. How about that one you want to send? Ready yet?"

Lowe pushed the blank pad back toward the operator. "I've changed my mind. Maybe later. I'm looking for a place to stay. Where did you say that boarding house was?

Thomas reached the main trail and picked up the pace. Apart from the wildlife, the only other hazards were the deep ruts from the wagons that ferried people and supplies from Valdez to points north. Riding down the middle was the best option if you didn't meet an oncoming wagon. With the recent rains, portions of the trail were slick. Thomas didn't push the horse too hard—the last thing he needed was a slip and fall.

The last couple of miles to Chicken were uneventful. Thomas let the horse take the lead—he was in no hurry. The day was warm, the leaves nearly fully covering the stands of alder and poplar. He was glad winter was over—the long dark days underground thawing and hoisting gravel grew old after a time. It was nothing but anticipation with no reward. The gravel might hold a fortune or nothing, but the answer lay frozen on the large dump, waiting for the day it met the sluice box. Thomas thought about the feast or famine nature of mining and wondered if it was all worth it. The summers could be filled with great reward—if not, the winter was all the more dismal.

The horse snorted and snapped Thomas back to attention. The town came into view, and he directed the horse to the telegraph office, hoping someone was there. He hopped off, and as he was wrapping the reins around the hitching post, Wayne came bursting out the office door, head down, apparently on a mission.

"Oh, didn't see you there," said Wayne as he nearly collided with Thomas.

"I noticed. Where you headed in such a hurry?"

Wayne stopped and pointed down the street. "Somebody found a pile of clothes behind the lumber mill. Got dried blood on 'em and looks like they're from the grave."

Thomas nodded. "I'll go with you."

They made their way to the reject pile at the back of the mill. The owner and one of his operators were looking down at the filthy pile of clothes, partially hidden in a pile of splintered, rough-cut timber. Thomas moved closer—the smell caused him to stop. The shirt and pants were in a heap next to a wool jacket shoved deep between two odd-shaped slabs of timber.

The mill owner poked the pile with a stick, moved the pants aside, then lifted the shirt up at arm's length.

"It's pretty much shredded."

"This is very odd," said Thomas. *What is going on here?*

"Whoever it was must have hidden here while they ripped this stuff up."

The pants were also shredded as if someone had taken a knife to them. Only the jacket looked to be relatively intact, with a rip here and there. The owner tossed the stick down in disgust.

"This is some sick business," he said. "Burn 'em."

The operator winced, then looked over the pile, hoping to find an unstained spot to grab. He gingerly picked up the shirt, then the pants, and took them to a nearby barrel used to burn garbage. He returned and grabbed the collar of the jacket and pulled—it was stuck. Cursing, he jerked harder on it to no avail, then grabbed with both hands and pulled. A loud ripping sound resulted, but the jacket sprung free. He turned towards the barrel, dragging the jacket behind him.

"Stop, hold on a second," said Thomas.

The operator turned and looked at him. "Why?"

"There's something in that seam," said Thomas, pointing at the freshly ripped area. Moving closer, he could see what it was—a stained, yellowed slip of paper, partially sticking out of the tear in the jacket.

"I ain't touching it," said the operator, dropping the jacket. "Got enough of this smell on me as it is."

Thomas reached down and gingerly pulled the folded paper from the seam.

"What is it?" said Wayne, who had been standing back, watching.

"Not sure," said Thomas as he unfolded it. "It's a single sentence."

"Could that be what the grave robber was looking for? A piece of paper?" said Wayne.

"I don't know, but if so, it doesn't make much sense."

Thomas shook his head and read it again.

Your Destiny lies on the NP befour you leave.

† † †

CHAPTER 5

John sat at the breakfast table, drumming his fingers and staring into the cup of coffee Stella just delivered. A week passed since he sent word to Seattle, and still no reply.

"Something wrong?" she asked.

John took a sip of the coffee without looking up. "No—maybe."

Stella sat down and waited.

"I'm just frustrated, waiting for word," he said. "I know I shouldn't care about the money—should have let it go, but for some reason, I can't."

"Is it because you aren't happy here? Not happy with me and our life?"

"Oh no," said John as he reached across the table and clasped her hands in his. "You know I love you and couldn't be happier you're my wife."

"Then what is it?"

"It just seems like unfinished business—something that tears at me as I think of all I've lost."

"So recovering your fortune would make it better?"

"It would be like closure. It would be as if Preston didn't win in the end."

"Well, he didn't win. He's dead."

"I know, but because of him, I lost my home, my fortune, my wife. I should never have trusted him."

Stella felt a sting at the mention of his wife. "You can't blame yourself for all that. From all you've told me, he came across as your friend."

"You can never tell about people. Everyone has something to hide—secrets."

"What's yours, John?"

Lowe sat on the horse along the trail, Stella's boarding house just barely in view through the trees. He kicked himself for the money wasted on the old nag, the cheapest transportation to be found in Valdez. *Should have just stolen a horse,* he thought, realizing that would deviate from his plan to keep a low profile. Lowe debated going straight up to the door and knocking but decided against it—for now.

He pulled out the telegram and reread it.

```
ERIK LOWE
VALDEZ, ALASKA

DONE HERE. AWAITING YOUR INSTRUCTIONS

/S/ A. FRIEND
CHICKEN, ALASKA
```

Very clever with the signature, thought Lowe. So his scruffy associate was finished in Chicken. Time to get on with it—he told A. Friend so in the telegram instructing him to meet at Wortman's Roadhouse. *Now we're getting somewhere.*

He put the telegram in his pocket, pulled his hat low, and nudged the horse forward. As he passed the boarding house, he looked for any sign of Palmer but saw no activity. He pushed the horse a little harder, hoping to make Wortman's before nightfall. He still had thirteen miles to go and didn't want to spend the night along the trail, having brought nothing along except a revolver, jacket, and a canteen of water. The early afternoon sun filtered through the trees that lined the trail, casting shadows that seemed to follow him as he passed.

He reached Keystone Canyon, a deep gorge formed by the Lowe River. His first thought was if one could survive a slip and fall into the torrent below. A shiver went up his spine, but he shook it off. He knew little of Wortman's but didn't expect much in the way of luxury—he was used to the dingy, dark hovels that passed for hotels in his past.

By the time he reached Wortman's, the sun was low in the sky, and he could feel the chill in the spring air. *Gonna be cold tonight.* He tied up the horse, taking note of the pole barn nearby, then surveyed the roadhouse. It was rather small, of log construction with a sloped roof made of milled lumber. Attached to the roadhouse through a separate entrance was a welcome sight—the *Klondike Saloon.* He wondered what kind of swill was served inside, but at least it would provide a distraction until his unkempt friend arrived on the stage from Chicken. Several small outbuildings surrounded the roadhouse, including a woodshed, a couple of cabins, and of course, the most important—an outhouse.

"Afternoon," said Lowe as he entered, his eyes adjusting to the dim light of the building. "I'm looking for a room."

The proprietor nodded. "We got one bed left if you want it, but it's in a room with two others."

Lowe winced at the thought of sharing a room, but

it wouldn't be the first time. Visions of the flophouses he drifted among before he finally clawed his way out of poverty flashed in his mind. He could deal with it, at least for a night.

"That's fine. Got a horse out there as well. Can you put her in the barn and get her some feed?"

"Sure, that'll cost you extra."

"Fine. Can I pay when I leave?"

The proprietor rubbed his chin. "Suppose so. When you leaving?"

"I'm waiting for the southbound wagon from Chicken to meet up with my partner."

"Ah, I see. It should be here tomorrow night at the latest. Maybe sooner, depending on the trail conditions up north."

"So one night, that'll be ten dollars and two more for taking care of your horse."

"Twelve dollars? Seems awful steep."

"You're welcome to go elsewhere," said the proprietor, a sneer spreading across his face.

"Fine. You got me over a barrel, so I'll take it."

"Room's that way," said the proprietor, pointing at a crude excuse for a door made from rough-cut lumber. There were gaps between the boards, and a chunk of moose antler served as a doorknob. There was no latch.

Lowe pushed the door open, revealing three beds, two of which were unmade. The third—his—consisted of a stained pillow and a single gray wool blanket. He sighed, then looked back at the proprietor. "Saloon open?"

"Always."

"I think I'll get a stiff drink, maybe several," said Lowe.

"Go ahead. That won't go on your tab so have your

money ready."

Lowe nodded and headed for the door. As he reached the saloon door, he heard the proprietor yelling at a boy to take care of the horse. A young fellow, probably no more than sixteen, came hurrying out the door, untied Lowe's horse, then led it to the pole barn. Satisfied, he reached for the saloon door and pulled it open. The smell of tobacco and stale whiskey assaulted his nose as his eyes worked to adjust to the dark interior. The pall of smoke hung low in the room as he approached the bar. In the corner were two tables, each occupied with several travelers working their way to a drunk.

"What'll it be, stranger?" said the bartender.

"Whiskey and keep 'em coming."

"Hope you brought your money. That's six bits a shot."

Lowe shook his head and slapped down several dollars. *Gonna be a long night, but hopefully, I won't remember it in the morning.*

Lowe raised up in bed and pulled his pocket watch out, struggling to focus—after nine in the morning. He pushed his fingertips deep into his forehead, then fell back on the bed, his head pounding with an epic hangover. He looked around the room—the other beds were unmade but empty. He wondered if they changed the sheets between guests, but the answer was obvious, judging from the stains. Sounds of conversation drifted in from the dining area of the roadhouse. He couldn't remember how he got back to the room, but one thing was sure—he needed coffee.

The dining area was just an open room off the main entrance. The furniture was rustic—all made from rough-cut lumber. Rather than chairs, benches lined the long tables. You had to be careful where you sat—otherwise, a jagged sliver was a real possibility.

The proprietor was standing near the entrance to what appeared to be the frontier version of a kitchen. Beyond, a short man with an overhanging belly stood stirring a pot of something, a big cigar drooping from his mouth. The proprietor looked at Lowe and laughed.

"Eh, you're alive."

Lowe scowled. "Barely. Can I get coffee?"

"Gonna need a couple gallons judging from your fun last night."

"I guess. I don't remember getting back to the room."

The proprietor laughed out loud. "The bartender and I dragged you in there after midnight. You passed out on the stool."

Lowe sat at an empty table, wanting only to nurse his hangover alone. The proprietor returned with a cup of coffee and set it down.

"Any chance of getting a shot of whiskey in there?"

"Hair of the dog, eh? I'll see what I can do. You hungry?"

"Not yet. Just coffee for now. Any idea when the southbound will arrive?"

"No, but probably this afternoon. You staying another night?"

He didn't like the prospect of spending another night, especially once his scruffy accomplice arrived. Valdez was still primitive by his standards but miles above a roadhouse on the trail. "Not sure. Depends on when it arrives."

He finished the cup of coffee, sans whiskey. *Some service.* The proprietor returned with the coffee pot in hand.

He refilled the cup. "Hungry yet?"

"I suppose. Never got my whiskey though."

"Oh. Sorry—got busy."

"Skip it. I need to have a clear head today. What's for breakfast?"

"You can have whatever you want, as long as it's beans and bacon."

"What—no eggs?"

"The chickens were a little stingy this morning, and you're late to the table."

Lowe grumbled. "Fine."

The proprietor grinned and headed back to the kitchen. Lowe pictured the beans stewing in the bottom of a crusty pot for weeks, just waiting for a victim. *Hope I'm not here for dinner,* he thought as his plate arrived.

"Dig in."

"Dare I ask what's for dinner if I have to stay over?"

The proprietor chuckled, gave him a look, and walked away.

† † †

It was mid-afternoon when John entered the Valdez telegraph office. After revealing his feelings about the money to Stella, the urge to come and check for a message became irresistible. On the trip to town, he tried to lower his expectations, beginning to think Stella was right—at some point, he would have to give it up and move on.

"Afternoon, Mr. Palmer," said the clerk. "Sending or expecting today?"

"Hoping for something from Seattle."

"I don't recall seeing anything for you, but I'll double-check."

The telegraph operator seated behind them shook his head, but no one noticed. The clerk began sifting through the message stack, slowly deciphering the names scribbled quickly by the operator as the messages came in. John was always amazed at the number of telegrams that passed through Valdez each day.

"Nothing for you, sorry."

"I figured as much," said John as he turned to leave.

"Say, did your friend find you?"

"Friend?"

"Yes, there was a fellow in here a day or so ago—can't remember exactly when. He came in right after you left and asked about you. Couldn't remember your name, so I told him, but he said he recognized you from Seattle."

Strange. "Did you catch his name?"

The clerk rubbed his chin and stared at the ceiling. "Uh, no. He told me, but I can't remember now. I'm not very good with names unless I see them on paper a few times."

John wondered how he could function in his job when he was poor with names. "What did he look like?"

"Oh, I don't know. Younger fella, brown hair, clean-cut but nothing fancy. Maybe in his mid-twenties."

"Did he say how he knew me or where he was staying?"

"Didn't say much, but did say he was looking for a place to stay. I told him about Stella's—thought maybe he would have showed up there."

"Nope. Anything else you can remember?"

"Not really, except he said he wanted to send a message but didn't. Seems to me like he just wanted to ask about you."

"Thanks," said John as he headed for the door. "If he comes in again, get his name for me, will you?"

"Sure. And I'll remember."

John unhitched the horse and mounted up. The horse waited, but he didn't nudge her on. *Who is this man, and what does he want?* The thought nagged at him as he re-played the faces and names that could match the sketchy description provided by the clerk. Nothing clicked, but he was suspicious. Perhaps it was one of his daughter's suitors—she had many that he scared away. Emily was always attracting the boys, but few made it past the first introduction.

He thought about asking at the hotel but decided against it. Spring always saw a large influx of people moving through town—staying a day or two then hitting the trail. Besides, there were plenty of places for a person to stay, especially if they had contacts. *A bit of mystery*, but Stella would have to know in case the young man showed up. The last time a young stranger showed up, at their wedding no less, it brought them close to disaster. *Not going to happen again.*

† † †

Lowe stood outside, leaning up against the wall and smoking a cigarette, when the southbound stage arrived. It was late afternoon, dashing his hopes of getting back to Valdez. It meant another night in the roadhouse, this time with Willy.

Calling it a stage was a bit of a misnomer. To most people, the word conjured up a vision of an enclosed coach. On the contrary, the Valdez-Eagle stage was an open wagon, wheeled in the summer and on skids in the winter. Riders were exposed to the elements, which at times made the journey most unpleasant.

Willy hopped off the wagon. "Hey, boss!"

Lowe winced and gave him a dirty look, which immediately registered with Willy. He frowned, grabbed his small pack from the wagon, and shuffled over to where Lowe stood.

"Watch your mouth. Come on," said Lowe, motioning for Willy to follow him around to the back of the saloon.

He made sure they were out of earshot, then turned to Willy. "Well, where is it?"

Willy wrinkled his brow. "Where's what?"

"The paper, you blasted idiot."

"I didn't find it."

Lowe cursed again, then slapped Willy across the face with an open hand. Willy stumbled backward, then took a haymaker swing, but missed, the momentum carrying him to the ground. Lowe kicked him in the side, and he let out a groan as the wind was knocked out of him.

"Get up, you stupid sod. Try that again, and there'll be a .45 slug in your brain."

Willy whimpered as he stumbled to his feet. Breathless, he struggled to speak. "I...I...tried, but...there was nothing...nothing there."

"What do you mean there was nothing? The letter clearly states the paper was hidden in the seam of Van Sant's clothes. Did you search thoroughly?"

Willy brushed himself off. "I ripped up the shirt and pants—found nothing."

"What about the coat? Was there a coat?"

"Yah, a wool one. The whole mess stunk so bad it

about made me sick."

"Forget about that. Did you look through the coat?"

"Well, sorta, but I heard a noise and got scared. It was getting close to daylight, so I stuffed it all in some boards and got out of there."

Lowe raised his hand again. Willy cowered, but the strike didn't come.

"Maybe somebody else already found it," said Willy, backing away.

Lowe shook his head, kicking himself for thinking a dolt like Willy could succeed at even the simplest task.

"What now?" said Willy.

"I'll figure something out."

"Sure would like a drink after that long time on the stage."

Lowe decided to not press the issue with Willy—time for that later. Time for a bit of compassion, even if it was put on. "Come on, let's get that drink."

Willy nearly ran to the door of the saloon, then waited for Lowe to catch up. He opened the door and entered, with Willy close behind. After falling off the barstool the night before, Lowe opted for sitting at an empty table. The bartender nodded as the pair entered and took a seat.

The bartender yelled at them across the room. "What'll it be?"

"Whiskey," said Willy. "And bring the bottle." He looked at Lowe. "You're paying, right?"

Lowe sighed, then pulled out a wad of money. "Guess so."

The bartender brought the bottle and two shot glasses. Without asking, he grabbed up the cash. "I'll give change if there is any."

Lowe folded his arms across his chest. "Should be

plenty there."

"We'll see," said the bartender as he walked away.

Willy had already downed two shots before Lowe could pour his first. Not wanting a repeat of last night, he decided to pace himself, knowing what was before him tomorrow. It didn't matter if Willy got soused—in fact, things could work out for the better that way.

"What's next...boss?" said Willy, his words already beginning to slur as the cheap alcohol invaded his brain.

"Don't call me boss. We're supposed to pretend to be partners."

Willy downed a shot and poured another. "Oh, good. That means I get an equal share of that big pot of money," he said, his voice rising above the din of the sparsely populated saloon.

"Shut up," Lowe growled, grabbing Willy by the arm and spilling whiskey on the table. He looked around, hoping no one was paying attention to them.

"What's a matter, boss? We're going to be rich when we find all that money."

Lowe leaned in close. "You're going to be dead if you don't shut up."

Willy grinned, his yellow teeth in full display. "I don't like you much. Maybe I'll kill you."

"You don't have the guts."

Willy ignored the comment and downed another shot. "You'll...never..."

"You were saying?" said Lowe, as he watched Willy's head bob up and down, then come to rest on the table.

The bartender came over and looked at Willy, picked up his head, and let it drop back to the table with a thud. He laughed. "Your friend had enough already."

Slam his head a few more times, thought Lowe before

he answered. "Yeah, he can't hold his liquor."

"You better get him to bed."

Lowe nodded and grabbed the bottle. "Can you help me?"

"Yeah, but where you going with that bottle?"

"I paid for it."

"Fair enough," said the bartender as he helped get Willy to his feet.

Lowe held him up with one hand and opened the door. With Willy between them, the pair dragged him from the saloon to the roadhouse.

"Let's drop him here," said Lowe, pointing at the floor next to his bed.

"Really? Gonna let him sleep it off on the floor?"

"I'm paying for the bed, so, yeah."

"Fine by me," said the bartender as he dropped Willy unceremoniously on the floor. He looked at the drunk on the floor and smirked. "You boys enjoy your evening."

Lowe shut the door behind him and looked at Willy passed out on the floor. The other two beds were empty but made up. Lowe presumed he had the room to himself for the night. *Decision time.* Willy was clearly a liability, couldn't keep his mouth shut, and was surely going to be a loose end when all was said and done.

He rolled Willy onto his back, held his mouth open, and started pouring. The liquid choked him, and Willy started gagging, spewing whiskey all over himself. *So much for that idea,* thought Lowe, realizing that trying to poison him wasn't going to work. Willy muttered something, coughed, then passed out again.

Lowe plopped into bed and lay awake for a long time, working out scenario after scenario, none of which ended well for Willy.

✝ ✝ ✝

CHAPTER 6

Lowe rose early, snuck out of the roadhouse, and saddled up the horse, hoping to get away before anyone noticed. Willy just stood there, eyes half open and barely conscious after his dance with whiskey the night before.

"Where's my horse?" said Willy with a loud voice.

"Quiet!"

"I don't have a horse," said Willy, his voice piercing the early morning stillness.

"We're going to double up. Now be quiet."

Willy coughed and spit on the ground. "I don't feel so good."

Lowe led the horse away from the barn and motioned for Willy to follow. They didn't get far.

"Going somewhere?" said the proprietor, a double-barrel shotgun leveled in their direction.

Lowe froze. "Uh...just getting ready to be on our way."

"I think you forgot something."

He hadn't forgotten anything. The plan all along was to stiff the proprietor and get free room and board. But, thanks to Willy and his yelling, that game was over.

"Oh...right," said Lowe. "Can you lower the scattergun?"

The proprietor lowered the gun but kept it at ready. "That'll be thirty-four dollars."

Lowe scowled at him. "Thirty-four? That's not right."

The shotgun raised just a little. "Oh, it's right. Twelve for you and your horse each night and ten for your friend's stay last night."

"He didn't even have a bed."

"Don't matter. He stays, he pays."

"I've paid less at real hotels in Seattle."

"Maybe all that whiskey messed with your head—you ain't in Seattle."

Lowe growled and dug out his wallet. He counted out the cash and thought briefly about throwing it on the ground in front of the man but decided against it. *Best to make him happy and get out of here.* "Here you go," he said, handing the money over.

"The proprietor counted it. "Should've charged you double for having to haul your hind end out of the bar."

Lowe bristled at the comment, but it wasn't worth a conflict.

The proprietor slung the shotgun over his shoulder and smiled. "Next time you're out this way, keep on going."

"Count on it," said Lowe as the man turned and walked away.

Willy raised his eyes wide open and chuckled, his head bobbing up and down with each laugh.

"What's so blasted funny?"

"Oh, nothing. He just told you what's what."

Lowe mounted up. "Shut up and get on the horse."

It took Willy several tries to clamber up on the horse. The first time he slid off her backside, causing her to stomp and spin around. He finally made it, then slid his arms around Lowe's waist.

"What are you doing, you idiot? Get your hands off me, or I'll leave you here."

Willy yanked his hands back. "How am I supposed to stay on then?"

"Grab hold of the back of the saddle. We're not going to be galloping down the trail, so it shouldn't be a problem."

Willy grabbed hold of the back of the saddle. "I guess that'll work."

Lowe shook his head and gently nudged the horse forward along the trail to Valdez.

Thomas sat at the table, nursing his morning coffee. He stared at the cryptic, wrinkled paper that lay before him—the note found in Van Sant's clothing. He read it for the hundredth time.

Your Destiny lies on the NP befour you leave.

He shook his head.

"Did you figure out what it means?" said Sdzeè as she joined him.

Thomas shook his head. "I have no clue. It seems silly, but someone thought it was important."

"Maybe the man that was looking for it knows what it means. Did anyone find out who he was?"

"No, I asked around but found out little, other than a stranger was in town for a day or so."

"Did you get his name?"

"Wayne, the telegraph operator, sent a message for him. He said his name was A. Friend."

"That is funny."

"Yes, he thought himself clever, but it wasn't that clever. Assuming he's the culprit, he must have something to hide apart from his grave-robbing activities."

"So now what will you do, Thomas?"

Thomas took another sip of coffee and drummed his fingers on the table. "Not sure, but it makes me wonder if there might be a clue in Van Sant's possessions."

"Where are they?"

"I can't remember what happened after he died. We took his body from our mining claim to town, but beyond that, I don't know."

"Did you look through his things at that time?"

"Yes, but we didn't dig through everything. I know there were a couple of guns, a wallet, and some other items."

"Well, someone must have his things."

"Unless they were thrown away. I'll have to check in town to see if I can find out."

Thomas looked again at the wrinkled note and wondered why Van Sant would sew it into the liner of his jacket. If it was important, surely he could remember that simple phrase. *No, it must be for someone else to find—but why?*

Thomas folded the note and slipped it into his pocket, wondering if solving this mystery was worth it. After all, there was nothing in it for him, but it could be important for John. *It's time to let him know.*

✝ ✝ ✝

Lowe stopped the horse at the edge of Keystone Canyon and dismounted. "Let's take a break."

"Good," said Willy. "My backside is killing me." He spit out a glob of tobacco, then wiped his mouth on his sleeve. "I think it's stupid you didn't get a horse for me."

Lowe ignored him and looked up and down the trail. He saw no one. He tied the horse off to a small tree and motioned to Willy. "Come on, let's sit over here on the ledge and have a smoke."

Willy nodded and followed, working on rolling a cigarette as he swayed his way to the ledge. "You know, I've been thinking. I don't think you're paying me enough."

"Oh?" said Lowe as he finished rolling a cigarette and lit up.

"Yeah. How much money did you say we're looking for?"

Lowe hesitated, then decided it didn't matter. "Upwards of seventy-five thousand dollars."

Willy tapped Lowe on the shoulder. "Whoa, that's a lot of money. So now that we're partners, it's a fifty-fifty split, right?"

Lowe stared at him. "Since when are we partners?"

Willy's demeanor changed—almost as if the bumbling dolt transformed into a conniving equal. "Since I know what you're up to and—well—if you don't cut me in, I'll louse up the whole deal."

Lowe gritted his teeth but held his tongue.

Willy took a drag on the cigarette and blew the smoke in Lowe's direction. "You know, now that I think about it, maybe it ought to be more like eighty-twenty."

Lowe laughed. "You can't be serious."

"Oh, I am. See, if you don't agree, you get nothing."

"And neither do you."

"No, I'll just take up the hunt myself."

Lowe looked out across the canyon a hundred feet

below. The river surged through the narrows, the water boiling and churning as it raced toward the sea. Finally, he looked back at Willy. "And you think I'm just going to sit by and let you do that?"

"Probably not," said Willy as he reached into his inside pocket, pulled out a .45 Colt, and laid it across his lap.

"Oh, you're going to shoot me?"

"No, not necessarily. All depends on if you go along."

"I don't think you're smart enough to go this alone."

Willy snarled, "I'm smart—plenty smart."

"Yeah, you really proved that in Chicken."

Willy picked up the Colt and turned it toward Lowe. "That wasn't my fault. I told you. The paper's not there."

"Looks like you got me over a barrel then," said Lowe as he stood up.

Willy got on his feet and turned toward him, .45 still raised. "So we have a deal?"

"I guess. Shake on it?" said Lowe as he extended his hand.

Willy nodded, shoved the Colt in his belt, and extended his hand. Lowe yanked hard, slugged him in the face with his free hand, then pushed. Willy screamed as he lost his balance on the ledge, then dropped to all fours to keep from going over. Lowe kicked him hard in the stomach, knocking the air out of him. Willy tried to stand, but Lowe kicked him repeatedly until finally, he collapsed, trying to breathe.

"You broke my ribs," he said between gasps.

"You started it, but it doesn't matter. I wasn't going to let you live anyway."

Willy struggled to pull the Colt from his belt, but he wasn't quick enough. Lowe kicked it free from his trembling hand, and it tumbled across the rocks out of reach.

"You're done—never should have trusted you in the first place."

Willy's eyes widened with fear, then caught enough breath to let out one final scream as Lowe shoved him over the edge. He watched as Willy smashed into the rocks below and bounced into the raging torrent. He watched as the current swept him away, then picked up the .45 and slowly returned to the horse, a thin smile across his face.

† † †

Not getting any sluicing done at this rate, thought Thomas as he arrived in Chicken. The whole issue with Van Sant was becoming a distraction, but it still worried him. He hoped for answers—perhaps for a key to the strange phrase found in Van Sant's clothes. Unsure where to start, he stopped at the telegraph office, thinking Wayne may know something.

"Greetings Thomas, what can I do for you today?" said Wayne.

Thomas was surprised—most times, Wayne was somewhere other than the telegraph office. "I wanted to ask you about Van Sant."

"Not sure I know any more than you do."

"Do you know what happened to his belongings after we brought his body to town?"

Wayne rubbed his chin. "Boy, I'm not sure. Didn't have much, did he?"

"Not really as I remember. A couple of guns, a wallet, and some miscellaneous items."

"Well, the fellas that buried him might know."

"Who was it?"

"I don't know all of them, but since we don't have a real undertaker in town, I think it was one of the lumber mill employees and maybe a couple of miners from out of town."

Thomas knew chasing around trying to find which miners were involved would take more time than he could afford. The mill employee was his best bet. "Thanks, I'm going to head to the mill."

At the mill, Thomas shouted to no avail, trying to get the operator's attention over the sound of the saw. He tried waving, but that didn't work either. He was about to climb up on the equipment when he felt a tap on his shoulder. Turning, he saw the mill owner motioning him to follow.

"What can I do for you?" said the owner once they were far enough away from the saw.

"I'm trying to find one of the men who buried Preston Van Sant."

"Why?"

"Well, with all the funny business at the grave, I'm looking into what happened to Van Sant's possessions after he was killed."

"I can answer that for you. When you and Palmer brought his body to town, I collected his things and turned them over to the post office for safekeeping—in case anyone ever came to claim them."

"Thanks. I'm going to see if I can take a look at them."

"What do you hope to find?"

"I'm not sure, but maybe some answers as to why someone would bother to dig him up."

Thomas left the mill and, on the way to the post office, stopped at the telegraph office.

"I need to send a telegram," he told Wayne as he entered.

Wayne shoved the pad and pencil over the counter to him. "Here you go."

Thomas started to write, then stopped. He hated trying to explain to John what was going on in a few cryptic sentences. Besides, anything he wrote was bound to be seen by several people along the way, and the Valdez office was known for spreading everybody's business around town. He tore up the message and started over.

```
JOHN PALMER
VALDEZ, ALASKA

I HAVE NEWS CONCERNING OUR LATE
NEMESIS.

TOO MUCH TO EXPLAIN. WILL SEND
DETAILS IN A LETTER.

/S/ THOMAS
CHICKEN, ALASKA
```

Thomas handed the message to Wayne.

"Whoa, that's pretty mysterious," said Wayne as he counted up the words. "What's it all about?"

Thomas shook his head. "I'll let you know when I know."

"That sounds even more curious."

"Just send it, please," said Thomas as he slapped down a couple of bills and waited for change.

"Oh...uh...sure. Right away."

Thomas left and continued on his way to the post office. He regretted sending a cryptic message to John but wanted to warn him to be on the lookout for his letter. Hopeful to find Van Sant's belongings, Thomas entered the small, two-room log cabin that served as the post office. It was barely a couple of years old and usually staffed only when mail arrived via the stage line. Still, it provided better privacy than the telegram offices.

Thomas closed the door and looked around. A small wood stove stood in the corner next to a short bench. The room was divided by a counter between the bench and the array of slots on the wall. On the counter was a bell. Around the corner, a door led to the other room. Thomas wasn't sure the purpose of the room but assumed it was a storage area. No one was around, but he heard a faint sound coming from the other room. He considered ringing the bell but stopped and listened. The sound of slow breathing reached his ears.

He stepped quietly around the counter and peered through the open doorway into the room. As his eyes adjusted to the dim light, he saw a small side table, a chair, and a cot. On the other side of the room were two cabinets stretching from floor to ceiling. On the cot was a woman, asleep and breathing lightly. He recognized her as a daughter of a local miner but couldn't remember her name. She wasn't there the last time he visited the post office, but apparently, she had taken over the mail duties. He backed out quietly, moved around the counter, and rang the bell.

He heard rustling and a cough. "Just a minute. I'm coming."

Thomas waited, and shortly the woman came through the door, smoothing the wrinkles from her clothes. She stood behind the counter, straightened her curly red hair, then said, "Whew. What can I do for you?"

Thomas looked at the smiling face with sparkling green eyes and freckles that ran across the bridge of her nose. He guessed she was probably close to thirty years old.

"Are you in charge of the post office now? I don't remember seeing you here before."

"I'm filling in here for a while—well, maybe permanently, I don't know. My name is Anna."

"What happened to the other fella?"

"Oh, he heard about the gold rush over at Nome and took off like a crazed coyote. I guess he's going to mine the beach and get rich."

Thomas laughed, knowing gold rush dreams often turned into nightmares. "Well, good luck to him, I guess."

"You're Thomas Thornton, aren't you?"

"That's right. How did you know?"

"I've seen you around town, but we've never been introduced."

"Well, glad to meet you, Anna."

Anna smiled, then did her rendition of a curtsy. "I don't recall seeing any mail for you. Are you sending something?"

Thomas hesitated. "Uh, well, no. I'm actually here looking for something else."

"Like what?"

"Do you know of the incident involving Preston Van Sant?"

"Of course. You can't keep something like that secret in a small mining town."

"Well, I'm looking for his belongings. The mill owner said they were stored here in case someone came to claim them."

Anna scratched her head, then smoothed her hair again. "I'm not sure. I haven't seen anything like that, but I haven't gone through everything either. I've been getting used to the job and, to be honest, trying to organize this place—was kind of a mess when I took over."

"Mind if I look around?"

"I suppose, but I don't think I can let you have his things."

"I just want to look."

Anna nodded. "Let's take a look in the cabinets in the back room. I've already been through most of the stuff here. What are we looking for?"

Thomas followed her into the other room. "Nothing in particular. I just want to have a look and see if there's anything that will solve a mystery for me."

"A mystery? I love mysteries. Have you read *The Turn of the Screw*? Quite a lovely novella."

"Haven't heard of that one," said Thomas, not wanting to admit he had little time for reading.

"It's by Henry James—more of a horror story, but fun all the same. It's about a young governess in England that—"

"Sorry, I'm sure it's a wonderful story, but I'm in a bit of a hurry."

"Oh, silly me. I get carried away by my books. Perhaps we could discuss it another time—and I could make dinner for you."

Thomas blushed—hoping she didn't notice. "Uh, I really need to take a look in the cabinets—and get back to my wife."

"Oh...wife." She stiffened, and the smile left her face. "Go ahead and look."

Thomas opened the first cabinet and found stacks of envelopes, a postmark tool, and miscellaneous odds and ends haphazardly tossed onto the shelves. Dust flew as he picked through the items, none of which had anything to do with Van Sant. He closed the cabinet door and opened the next one. It was empty except for an open wooden box on the bottom shelf. It appeared to once hold explosives—the *Dupont* emblem was stamped on each side. Scratched in the faded wood were the initials PVS.

Thomas slid the box out, picked it up, and sat it on the counter in the main room.

Anna peered over the edge of the box. "Is that it? What's in it?"

Thomas didn't say anything. On top were some dusty, half-folded clothes—a shirt and folded pair of pants. He removed them and set them on the counter. Van Sant's revolver was in the box, but his rifle—the one he tried to kill John with—wasn't. Thomas removed the gun and a box of ammo next to it. What remained was a scarf, wrapped up in a bundle. Thomas picked it up and un-rolled it on the counter, revealing two wallets—one black and the other in brown leather. He had forgotten about the second wallet, something that he and John wondered about at the time of Van Sant's death.

"Not much," said Anna. She leaned closer to Thomas. "Do you think there's money in there?" she said in a hushed voice.

He wasn't sure why she was whispering, but he wasn't interested in money. He opened the black wallet and found no money. It was nearly empty except for a faded photograph of a family—man, woman, and child, and a stub from a steamer ticket bearing the name of Charlie Wilson.

Thomas held up the stub. "I remember this."

"Oh?"

"Yes, this wallet appears to belong to a fellow named Charlie Wilson. His belongings were in with Van Sant's, but we never knew who he was. I guess that will remain a mystery."

"Anything else in that one?"

"No." Thomas placed it back in the box, then opened the leather wallet, which he assumed belonged to Van Sant. Any money that Van Sant had was long gone. The wallet was surprisingly empty—no pictures or identification. The only way Thomas was sure it belonged to Van Sant was the letters *V S* embossed on the outside.

"Nothing good in that one either?" said Anna.

"No money if that's what you're thinking."

Thomas lifted a flap, revealing a small pocket. In it was a single, folded piece of paper. He removed it, unfolded it, and read.

DH&C 6836

"What's that?" said Anna.

"Just a slip of paper. Doesn't seem to mean anything."

Anna snatched it out of his hand and read it. "Humph," she said as she dropped it on the counter.

Thomas searched the rest of the wallet and found nothing. He was pretty sure that at some point, the wallets had been looted. The remnants of Van Sant's life amounted to a pair of clothes, a revolver, and an empty wallet.

"Did you find what you're looking for?"

"No, but I'd like to take the clothes with me. No one's going to want those. We can put the rest back."

"Why do you want the clothes?"

Thomas didn't want to tell her the real reason. "Uh, I think they'll fit a friend of mine that's down on his luck. No point in letting them rot away here, is there?"

"No, I guess not."

Thomas folded the shirt and placed it on the counter, covering the slip of paper. He did the same with the pants, then rolled the two together, making sure the slip of paper ended up within.

"I'll put this back for you," he said.

"No, that's fine, Thomas. I can handle it."

"Okay, thanks. I'll be back in a day or so with a letter to mail."

"Better make it tomorrow if you want it to go out soon. The stage from Eagle is supposed to be here tomorrow, and the mail will be going with it."

Thomas nodded and tucked the rolled-up clothes under his arm, then turned to leave.

"Oh, Thomas."

"Yes?"

"Tell me about your wife. I don't know her."

Thomas frowned but erased it from his face before he turned back to Anna.

"I thought everyone around here knew Sdzeè."

"Oh...Sdzeè. I know her but didn't realize you were the one she married. I just got back this spring after wintering in the south. I heard she married last fall but didn't get the details."

"Yep, I'm the one."

Anna took a step towards him and looked up at him. "Tell me, Thomas, truly. Are you happy?"

Thomas took a step back.

"I mean marrying a girl like her, I can't help but wonder."

"What do you mean?"

"You know..."

Thomas fumed but hid it. He knew exactly what she

meant and wanted to tell her it was none of her business but decided not to risk angering her. He didn't want her throwing his mail in the trash. "Yes, we're very happy."

She picked up the box and turned away. "Oh, I see. Well, goodbye then," she said as she entered the back room.

† † †

Thomas sat at the table, pencil in hand, staring at the blank piece of paper. The ripped-up remains of Van Sant's clothes sat in a heap next to him. On the trip home from the post office, he thought about how to explain the situation to John, but now the words failed him.

Sdzeè put a cup of coffee in front of him and sat down. "What is wrong?"

"I'm not sure what to put in the letter. I don't want to alarm John, but this all seems very strange."

"What makes you think it has anything to do with John?"

Thomas put down the pencil and took a swig of coffee. "Maybe it doesn't. Just doesn't seem random to me. Of all the graves in the cemetery, why dig up that one? Whoever it was must have been desperate to find something—something they thought was buried with Van Sant."

"And you think that piece of paper with the odd words is it?"

"Could be. Or maybe they were looking for something else—I don't know what to think."

"What of these clothes?"

"I thought perhaps there were more secret notes. That's why I wanted to search them."

Sdzeè picked up the shredded shirt, its seams all ripped and hanging in tatters. She did the same with the pants, then laughed.

"What's funny?"

"Oh, you'll never be able to wear these now."

Thomas smiled. "Very funny. I guess that was a pointless exercise."

Sdzeè nodded, then picked up the slip of paper found in Van Sant's wallet. "And what does this mean—another mystery?"

"I don't know what it means either, but I'm going to mention it in the letter—that and the mysterious phrase. John can take it from there."

Sdzeè put the slip of paper down and got up from the table. "I'm going to see if the chickens have laid anything today."

Thomas nodded and watched her leave the cabin. He picked up the pencil and started to write, laying out the scene at the cemetery, the note found in Van Sant's coat, and the slip of paper from his wallet. The letter ended with him suggesting all of it could mean nothing—had nothing to do with them. He signed the letter, folded it, and placed it in an envelope. *Too late to mail it today.*

Sdzeè returned, carrying a couple of eggs in one hand. "Chickens were lazy today. Did you finish the letter?"

"Yes, now all I have to do is mail it, something I'm not looking forward to."

"Why?"

"The person at the post office makes me a little uncomfortable."

Sdzeè tipped her head and looked at him with one eye. "And why is that Thomas Thornton?"

"It's that woman Anna."

"Oh?"

"She's a little—how would you say—aggressive."

Sdzeè laughed and patted Thomas on the back. "Oh, Anna—the little redhead. She is always husband-hunting. You better watch out. She might get you."

"It's not funny."

Sdzeè looked at him, her cheeks puffed out, then burst into laughter again. "Oh, but it is. You are so cute when you are embarrassed."

"I still don't think it's funny."

"Do you want me to come along and protect you?"

Thomas jumped up from the table, growling in feigned anger, then locked her in a big bear hug. She laughed, broke free, and pushed him away.

Thomas grabbed both her hands and stared into her eyes. "Do I look like I need protecting?"

"No, Thomas. But sometimes you need rescuing."

"I can live with that. I'll go see the little redhead tomorrow."

Sdzeè wagged her finger at him. "Don't make me come rescue you."

CHAPTER 7

Erik Lowe sat in the lobby of the Valdez hotel, smoking a cigarette and reading the newest edition of the Seattle Times. Newest was a bit of a misnomer—it was already over a week old when it arrived on the latest steamship. Though brief, it still provided an escape from his current situation. After Willy failed to find anything on Van Sant's body, Erik had to reconsider his options. He knew the money was more than likely still hidden—still waiting to be discovered. Unfortunately, he had little to go on.

Willy could have done more—could have made inquiries into what happened to Van Sant's belongings, but knowing him, he would have made a mess of it. Now the answer was either in Chicken or Valdez. *Two ways to play it,* he thought. He could go to the roadhouse as a guest and hope to learn what he needed to know. There was an off chance that he could be recognized, but he looked different now. His dark brown hair was shoulder-length, and the broad mustache that graced his upper lip made him look older—much older than anyone at the roadhouse would remember.

The other option was the brute force method. To take Palmer and make him talk. He could remember little of the man, nor how he would react to such a tactic. Unlike many in the game, Lowe preferred the intelligent approach—the long con. It was less messy when it worked and often meant one could escape without the mark even knowing they had been taken. *It's worth the risk.* Besides, if he was found out, there was always the other option.

He made his way to the counter and slapped the bell, even though the clerk had already seen him.

"Can I help you?"

Lowe nodded. "I need to check out."

"Your name?"

Erik just stared at him.

"I need your name."

"Seriously? You know who I am."

"Yes, Mr. Lowe. But it's a formality."

He shook his head and slapped the room key on the counter. "The room's unlocked. I'm going up to get my things. If you want to get paid, stop the nonsense."

The clerk sighed. "Just trying to class the establishment up a bit, sir."

"I think you should try something else instead of annoying your paying guests."

"Sorry. I'll have your bill ready when you come down from the room."

Annoyed, Erik didn't acknowledge the clerk but made his way to the room. He had brought few possessions with him to Alaska—it didn't take long to pack his bag with clothes, revolvers, ammo, and the other few odds and ends. He dragged the bag downstairs, dropped it by the door, then went to the counter.

The clerk didn't say anything but slid the bill across the counter. Erik looked it over. "Seems right."

The clerk nodded. "We do our best."

Somehow Erik wasn't sure that was the case. "Let

me ask you something."

"Certainly."

"What can you tell me about Stella's boarding house?"

"Not a lot. It's certainly not as upscale as our hotel."

"Well, I'm thinking of staying there on my way north. What about the owners?"

"Oh, they'll treat you right. Stella has been here for years, and her new husband is an okay fellow."

"That's good to know. That's John Palmer, right?"

"That's right."

"I read somewhere he had a bit of trouble with a former friend."

"Oh. The Van Sant affair. Yes, that was quite the to do."

"Do you know details?"

"You seem quite curious."

"Just a passing interest."

"Well, as you most likely read, Van Sant embezzled all of Palmer's money from the bank in Seattle, burned his house, and ran off with his wife."

"Not all of that was in the papers."

"No, guess not. And that's not the half of it. He came here looking for Palmer, followed him to Chicken, and attempted to murder him. But, of course, it didn't work out that way. Palmer's partner killed him, and that was the end of it."

So far, none of it was new to Erik. The papers reported most of it, and he knew the rest. No one seemed to have the answers he wanted. Odds were the clerk wouldn't know, but it was worth a try. "What happened to all of Van Sant's belongings?"

The clerk shrugged. "I don't know. Never heard anyone talk about that. Seems like an odd question."

Erik saw he was getting nowhere and may have created suspicion, though he wasn't sure the clerk was anyone to worry about. "Thanks," he said as he paid the bill.

"Good luck up the trail."

Erik picked up his bag, opened the door, and left without saying a word. The horse sidestepped as he mounted up. He slapped the reins across her rear, and she took off down the street, drawing looks from the people along the way. The town faded into the background, giving way to the trail along the river. He kicked himself for asking the clerk about Van Sant. *Have to be more clever in the future.*

The boarding house was roughly five miles out of town, and he slowed the horse to a walk, giving him time to work on a convincing story. He had to be more careful if he was to get the information he needed. *I just hope I recognize it when I find it.*

† † †

Thomas arrived early at the post office, hoping to get there before the mail pickup. He thought about asking Sdzeè to come along in case he needed help escaping, but that meant hitching up the wagon. Sdzeè told him not to bother, assured him he could handle the little redhead, and waved him on.

He hitched the horse and stared at the closed door of the post office, letter in hand. He wasn't sure about Anna—she seemed both pushy and insulting. At his initial visit, he made it clear that he was a happily married man—at least he hoped the message was received. He waited, still looking at the door. *I could just slip it under the door,* he thought. Suddenly he wished Sdzeè had come along—or better yet, that she mailed the letter.

The door opened, and out stepped Anna, her long, wavy red hair going every which way. "Well, are you going to come in or just stand there? I've been watching you for five minutes."

Thomas didn't think it was five minutes, but then again, it could have been. *This is stupid,* he thought as he headed up the steps.

"I was thinking," he said as Anna stepped aside and he entered.

"That's what I like—a thinking man."

Here we go again, thought Thomas as he watched her sashay around the end of the counter and take up her official position. She leaned forward, elbows on the counter, and looked up at him.

Thomas placed the letter on the counter. Anna didn't look at it but rather continued her upward gaze.

"Uh...I need to...mail this."

Anna straightened up, then picked up the letter. "Valdez. Hmm...and to John Palmer. How's he doing? Him and his new wife?"

Thomas started to roll his eyes but caught himself. "They're doing fine."

"Oh, good. So, what did you have to say in the letter?"

Thomas furrowed his brow. *Was she serious?* He wondered how many of the letters that came through the post office she ended up reading. He waited, not saying anything, lest words best left unsaid escaped from his mouth.

Anna stamped a postmark on the letter. "Well, then. I guess we'll just get on with it."

Thomas relaxed his gaze. "Will that make it out today?"

"Yes. As long as you pay the postage."

Thomas did so, then turned to leave.

"Oh, Thomas..."

Not again.

Anna moved from around the corner and caught up with him at the door. She smiled and moved between him and the exit. "You know that dinner offer still stands."

"My wife and I would love to attend, but we're really busy at the mine right now."

Anna's smile faded. "I see," she said as she stepped aside, her eyes locked on his.

"Thank you," said Thomas as he stepped outside. The door closed behind him, and he drew a sigh of relief. *She's a busybody for sure.*

† † †

At mid-morning, Erik stopped short of the boarding house. Still unsure of how to play it, he rolled a cigarette, then let the horse graze while he smoked. He dreamed up a story—having saved up enough money to come to Alaska, he was now headed north to the goldfields. A stay at the boarding house was needed to establish a rapport and hopefully get the required information. To that end, he was "waiting" for his partner to arrive from the states—a total fabrication.

Satisfied he had a workable story, he tossed the cigarette on the ground, stamped it out, and mounted up. The boarding house was just around the bend—the only concern now was if Palmer would recognize the face that had changed so much over the years. If so, the game was up, and he would have to resort to a plan that involved violence—something that he found oddly satisfying. *Willy could be just the beginning.*

The boarding house came into view, a two-story building made from milled lumber. It had a weathered coat of white paint, a porch that extended along the front, and a set of steps leading to the front door. Erik passed it before on his way to Wortman's but didn't pay close attention to it. After Wortman's, it looked quite civilized—perhaps even comfortable. There were no horses tied to the rail, a sign that there were no other guests—at least he hoped so. It would make his work easier. He would have the run of the place, making searching easier—if it came to that. He tied up the horse, noting the barn beyond the house and a chicken coop nearby. He cared little for animals—if he could get someone else to take care of the nag, it would relieve him of a mundane but necessary task.

Erik walked up the steps and stopped. There was a sign next to the door that read:

STELLA'S BOARDING HOUSE
W E L C O M E

He took that as an invitation to walk in, but to be safe, he knocked twice and waited. Footsteps approached, and the door opened to reveal a slender woman with salt and pepper hair. She was nearly as tall as him, and though she looked delicate, something told Erik she could hold her own. He guessed her to be in her early fifties.

"Can I help you?" said Stella.

He extended his hand. "Derik Tannvas. I'm looking for a place to stay while waiting for my partner to arrive."

She shook his hand and smiled. "I'm Stella, and it just so happens you're in luck. We have plenty of vacancies at the moment."

He returned the smile. "Wonderful."

"Get your things, and I'll show you to a room. Dinner is promptly at six each evening."

"And breakfast?"

Stella laughed. "Yes, we serve you breakfast starting at seven and can fix lunch for you as well—it's all the same price."

"Sounds great. I'll get my things."

Erik fetched his bag from the horse and smiled to himself, pleased with the deception—and the new alias, one he considered particularly clever. He returned and entered to find Stella waiting for him. "You run this place by yourself?"

"Oh, no. I used to when my first husband passed, but I recently remarried."

"Oh, congratulations. So will I get to meet your husband?"

"Yes, he's around somewhere. Probably out girdling trees."

"Girdling?"

"Yes. We remove the bark from around the tree and let it stand. By the next year, it becomes standing dry firewood. Then we—well, my husband—cuts it down and hauls it in."

"That's interesting, but it sounds like work."

Stella smiled at the city boy. "Everything out here is work."

"Guess so. Is it possible to get care for my horse as well?"

"Yes, we have room in the barn and can make sure she's fed and watered."

Derik nodded, then stood, still holding the bag.

"Let's get you to your room. That bag looks heavy. Follow me."

Stella led him up the creaking stairs to a hallway lined with narrow doors, each room marked with the name of a local flower or animal. She opened the second door on the left.

"Here we are. You'll have the Fireweed room."

"Fireweed?"

"Yes. Aren't you familiar with it?"

"No, not really."

Stella took his bag and placed it on the bed. "Fireweed is a plant that grows in clearings, especially after a forest fire. It's a tall, single stock with magenta flowers that work their way to the top as they bloom. Once they reach the top, winter's on its way."

"Really?"

"Well, that's the folklore anyway."

"Interesting. When will I get to meet your husband?"

"At dinner. Perhaps you'd like to rest?"

Derik nodded, even though he wasn't tired. "I'll just unpack a couple of things and relax for a bit."

Stella reached the door. "Okay. If you need anything, let me know."

"Thanks. And it's nice to meet you."

"Same here," said Stella as she gently pulled the door closed.

Derik sat on the bed and looked out the window. *So far, so good, but the real test comes at dinner.*

Derik checked his pocket watch. *Nearly six.* He looked in the small mirror that hung on the wall of the Fireweed room. He combed his hair, then carefully groomed the bushy mustache that graced his upper lip. *Perhaps I should have grown a full beard.*

Satisfied, he slowly opened the door and listened. He could hear noises downstairs but couldn't discern their origin. He stepped out into the hall and listened again. The sound of voices became clear—male and female. Since he was the only guest at the moment, he assumed it was Stella and her husband. He shivered, a wave of anxiety sweeping over him. If he was recognized, the game was over. Resolve replaced anxiety as he closed the door and started for the stairs.

John Palmer was seated at the dining table, smoking a pipe and reading what appeared to be an edition of the *Seattle Times*. Derik paused on the stairs as John turned to look at him.

John stood and extended his hand. "You must be Derik. Come on down and join me. Stella almost has our dinner ready."

Derik cleared the last step and clasped John's hand firmly. "Nice to meet you."

"Likewise. Have a seat."

Derik took the chair across from John and settled in. He scanned his face but saw no initial sign of recognition.

John sat down and scooted his chair up close to the table. "Have we met? You look familiar."

Derik shifted his weight in the chair, struggling to maintain his composure—that neutral look that he had practiced so often. "I don't believe so."

John shrugged, then glanced toward the kitchen where Stella was busy dishing up food for the table. "I'm getting pretty hungry," he said, raising his voice.

Stella didn't turn to look at him, just waved her hand over her shoulder. "Patience."

John laughed. "She loves it when I nag her."

"Right," said Stella, still busy plating food.

John returned to his pipe. "So, where are you from, Derik?"

"Uh...Seattle mostly."

"I hail from Seattle. Lived there for years before coming to Alaska."

"You planning to ever go back?"

John shook his head. "Not sure. Nothing there for me, really."

"Oh?"

"It's a long story, one I'd rather not go into."

Derik nodded, his first attempt at getting John to open up at an end. "Understand."

Stella brought plates heaped with mashed potatoes smothered in gravy and a large slab of beef steak. She placed them on the table. "I'll be back with silverware."

"Thanks, dear," said John.

Stella returned with the utensils and a plate for herself. "Sorry about the steak. Normally I'd serve you authentic Alaska fare, but we're out of moose meat."

Derik cut a large chunk from the steak, stuck a fork in it, and raised it. "Steak's fine with me—never had moose. You raise your own beef?"

"No, the steamships bring in fresh beef weekly now."

"Very civilized." Derik shoved a bite in his mouth.

"Yes, getting more so every day," said Stella.

Derik suffered through the small talk as the meal went on. Finishing the last bite of steak, he decided to carefully broach the subject again. "So I read in the Seattle papers there was a bit of trouble up here."

Stella looked at John, who was now staring into his plate. "Oh?"

"Something about a shootout up north a year or two

ago," said Derik, hoping he wasn't pushing too hard too fast.

John looked up from his plate and stared at Derik, then stood. "I'm done. Going to close up the barn for the night."

Derik watched him go out the back door. "Was it something I said?"

"It still pains him. Best not to bring it up," said Stella.

"I'm sorry. Can you tell me why? I know some of it."

Stella sighed. "His friend and lawyer stole all his money, burned his house, and ran off with his wife. And, after all that, followed him here to murder him."

"But he ended up getting it instead?"

"Yes, but not before John's daughter was killed in the crossfire. That's the whole story. Please leave it at that."

Derik nodded, unhappy with learning nothing that would help him further. "I understand."

Stella stood and collected the empty plates from the table, then turned to Derik. "Thank you."

"Sure," said Derik. "Thank you for dinner. I hope John doesn't hold my insensitive curiosity against me."

"He's not the type," said Stella as she retreated to the kitchen.

† † †

CHAPTER 8

Derik sat on the edge of the bed, fully dressed, and struck a match, struggling to read the time from his pocket watch. The night was moonless and clear—as dark as could be—no light filtered through the window. The match flickered and went out. He cursed and lit another, finally able to read the time—an hour after midnight.

He had slept little, checking the time often and waiting until he could begin. Searching the house in the dark wasn't ideal, but perhaps the only way. He assumed that Stella was almost always present, so the chance to search during the day was remote. It was almost futile, but his goal was two-fold—find out if Palmer had the money and, if not, where Van Sant's belongings were.

He took the kerosene lamp from the bedside table and lit it, turning the wick down low so as not to be too bright. It was a risk walking around the house with a flickering light, but it couldn't be helped. He glanced at his boots on the floor next to the table but decided it would be quieter without them. He stood, lamp in his left hand, and slowly opened the door. It barely squeaked on the hinges. *So far, so good.*

He stepped slowly out into the dark hall and paused. Palmer's bedroom had to be on this floor, but he wasn't sure which room. It was too risky to snoop around their room while the couple was sleeping—that would have to wait until another time. He moved toward the stairs and started down. The first step groaned under his weight, and he froze. Though he'd been up and down several times since arriving, the creaking stairs didn't register until now.

He grabbed the handrail and pushed down hard, taking some of the weight off each step as he continued down. It helped, but in the stillness of the night, it seemed as though they screamed out his presence. He moved slower, finally reaching the bottom. Pausing, holding his breath, he listened—nothing.

Derik held the lamp high as he moved forward, through the living room and past the dining room to the kitchen. He hadn't been in this part of the house simply because it would have seemed odd to go past the common areas. The large wood-fired cooking stove took up much of the room. As he moved past, He felt the warmth still emanating from it, the embers still alive. Next to it was a wood box, half full of split firewood. An icebox sat in the corner, its wooden doors standing open. He held the lamp near, only to find it was used as a cupboard, with various cans and staples on its only shelf. *Nothing here.*

Above the stove, running the entire length of the room, were shelves stocked with more goods—coffee, canned fruit, dried beans, rice, flour, and more. He shook his head. *Not really a place to hide money,* he thought. He moved toward the back door and found a closed door to his left. He opened it slowly to reveal a cramped office with a rolltop desk—beyond that, another door. He paused again to listen, knowing that the creaking stairs would alert him to someone approaching. Still no sound from the floor above.

Derik slowly opened the rolltop desk to find various papers, a journal, and a guestbook. He set the lamp down, then quickly flipped through the journal and guest book, looking for anything hidden between the pages. Finding nothing, he began carefully shuffling through the stack of papers. Bills, orders, notes on dinner ideas—all rubbish—nothing he could use.

He picked up the lamp and opened the next door, revealing a set of rough wooden stairs leading down. He descended slowly, the lamp held out in front. Reaching the bottom, his eyes took a moment to adjust after lowering the light. He was in a root cellar, dug out under the house with simple log walls cut from small spruce trees. Crates of potatoes lined the wall, and groups of winter squash were placed carefully on shelves of rough-cut lumber. The smell was earthy, damp, and cool. He sighed. *Another dead end.*

He ascended the stairs and pulled the door closed. It made a loud click as the latch caught. He grimaced, then moved forward to the kitchen. The flickering of light against the wall of the dining room caught him by surprise. He took a step, and the sound of a round being jacked into the chamber of a lever action rifle echoed from the dining room. He froze—waiting.

The lamp grew brighter, slowly approaching.

"Come out with your hands in the air."

He panicked—caught, with only one hope. "Uh, just me," he called out softly as he approached the source of the light in the dining room.

"Come out now, or you won't live to regret it."

Derik rounded the corner, hands in the air, the lamp dangling high above his head. There stood John, the .44-40 carbine leveled in his direction.

"What do you think you're doing?" said John.

Derik managed a weak laugh. "Don't shoot me. I got hungry and was just looking for a snack and something to drink."

John stared at him, trying to read him in the dim light of the lamp. He lowered the carbine. "Good way to get yourself killed."

"Sorry, I thought it would be okay."

John set the carbine and lamp on the dining room table. "We get rough customers through here from time to time. Never know when it's going to turn out bad."

"That's fine," said Derik. "I accept your apology."

John raised an eyebrow. "I wasn't apologizing, just stating a fact."

Derik felt the heat rising in his face, the urge to lash out threatening the plan. "I'm sorry."

"Don't worry about it. I'll have Stella send something with you after dinner so you'll have it in case you get hungry. It's been a while since I shot a guest—wouldn't want to repeat it this soon."

Derik couldn't tell if he was joking. *Anything's possible.*

John moved past him to the kitchen and grabbed a biscuit from a basket on the top shelf. "Here," he said, handing it to Derik. "This should tide you over till breakfast."

Derik brushed past him and headed toward the stairs. "Thanks."

The sound of the carbine and lamp being retrieved from the dining room table reached Derik.

"One last thing," said John.

Derik shuddered and turned.

"There's a pitcher of water on the table in your room—in case you get thirsty again."

Derik nodded and started up the stairs. "G'nite—sorry again for the trouble."

John ignored him, already at the back of the kitchen, staring at the wide-open door to the little office and the rolltop desk. *Stella never leaves this open at night.*

Though only five in the morning, the sun was already peeking through the kitchen window. Stella shoveled heaping spoonfuls of coffee into the pot and paused, looking out the window. She smiled as the shadows slowly surrendered. It never ceased to amaze her at the amount of daylight in the north. It was astounding—eighteen hours of light in the summer and less than five in the depths of winter. She put the pot on the wood-fired stove and began slicing potatoes. Their one and only guest would likely be down for breakfast in an hour.

John shuffled into the dining room and plopped into a chair. "Coffee?"

Stella turned and looked at him, both hands firmly on her hips. "Good morning to you too, Mr. Palmer."

John rubbed his forehead. "Sorry. Was up in the middle of the night."

"Oh?"

"I heard a noise downstairs, so I went to investigate. Glad I didn't wake you."

"What was it?"

"I found our guest roaming around down here. He was in the kitchen when I caught up with him. I think I gave him quite a scare when he saw the business end of the carbine."

"What was he after?

"He said he was looking for something to eat, but I'm not sure I believe him."

"Why?"

"Did you notice the door to the office? And the desk?"

Stella shook her head, then turned to look. "Oh."

"Did you leave the door open last night?

"I don't remember."

"What about the desk? I thought you always kept the rolltop down when you weren't using it."

Stella rubbed her chin. "True, but I can't be sure."

"Well, that's my concern."

"Oh, John. You're going to ruin our business if you keep shooting the guests," said Stella, trying to keep a straight face.

John laughed, causing Stella to do the same. "You know I haven't shot anybody yet."

"Oh shoot!" said Stella as the pot boiled over, spewing coffee and grounds all over the stove. She grabbed a towel as the liquid sizzled and bubbled across the hot cast-iron surface. "Now look what you made me do—distracting me like that."

John laughed. "Sorry. I guess I'll have to wait longer for that first cup."

"If you get any at all."

"Seriously, I'm going to keep an eye on that fellow. I don't know if he was snooping or not, but if he's looking to rob us, we need to be on guard."

Stella's eyes widened. "I wonder..."

"What?"

She quickly looked back toward the stairs, then slid the wood box away from the wall.

"Oh," said John, realizing her concern.

Stella knelt and opened the small hatch near the floor, revealing a little shelf with two quart Mason jars. "Looks like everything is here," she said quietly, just as the distinct creaking of the stairs reached her ears.

Stella quickly closed the hatch, and John slid the wood box back in place. They turned to see Derik just reaching the last step, then looked at each other, silent.

"Good morning," said Derik as he joined them in the kitchen. He looked at John. "Sorry about last night."

John nodded, then noticed Stella standing conspicuously in front of the wood box. Behind her, he could see faint marks on the floor where the box had been slid out. He moved forward, put his hand on Derik's shoulder, and pointed him toward the dining room.

"Let's have a seat. Stella will have coffee for us shortly, and we can have a little chat."

Derik nodded. "Sounds good. Looking forward to coffee and breakfast."

Stella waited until they were seated in the dining room, then quickly shuffled over the marks on the floor. Satisfied they were no longer able to tell the tale, she set about repairing the coffee mess.

"Coffee will be ready in about five minutes. John, why don't you take Derik out to the chicken coop and collect some fresh eggs for breakfast."

John looked at him. "How about it? Give me a hand, and I'll show you around a bit while we're out there."

Derik yawned. "I guess—if you promise to have coffee for me when I return, ma'am."

"It'll be ready lickety-split," said Stella as she watched them head to the main door. "Don't be too long with the chickens."

She waited until the door closed behind them, then

entered the office. It looked like nothing was missing from the desk, but there was no way to know if things had been tampered with. She quietly shut the rolltop and returned to the kitchen, closing the door to the office.

† † †

John paused at the door to the chicken coop. "So, Derik, what brings you to our little slice of heaven?"

Derik shifted his weight. "Well, as I said, I'm waiting for my partner to arrive before heading north."

"And where are you headed once he shows up?"

"North."

"Sure, but where? Do you have a mining claim, or are you just prospecting? I noticed you don't have any gear with you."

Derik's face felt warm. He hoped it wasn't visible. He had a story, but it wasn't detailed or well thought out, and probably not defensible. He coughed.

"Well, actually, we are looking for a claim to purchase. Hopefully, one complete with everything needed to get started."

John looked at him sideways, then pulled his pipe and tobacco pouch from his pocket. He tamped the tobacco in, replaced the pouch, and then looked again at Derik who was now shuffling his feet in the dirt.

"Do I make you nervous?"

"Uh, a little. After all, you did pull a gun on me."

John lit the pipe, shook the match out, and tossed it on the ground. After a long draw, he said, "So you came up here without any real plans and don't know where you're going?"

"I know it sounds a little crazy, but isn't that what the early prospectors did?"

"Well, yes. But at least they came prepared. Seems you might be in for some trouble—you're a little green."

Derik bristled but did his best to hide it, trying to come up with an answer to put an end to the interrogation. "My partner is the expert. He's bringing along what we need."

"I see. Why didn't you come together?"

"Uh, he had some...uh things to deal with before he came."

"So you came ahead to—do what?"

His temper rising, Derik's mind raced, searching frantically for an out.

"I...well, you know—scope things out."

"I see. Let's get those eggs. Stella's waiting," said John as he opened the door to the coop.

Stella lifted the big cast-iron skillet from the overhead hook and placed it on the stove. She scooped two heaping lumps of lard into it, then tossed in the sliced potatoes. Bacon was in short supply, so eggs and potatoes would have to do today. *John needs to make a run to the store,* she thought as she tended to the sizzling skillet.

"Smells good," said John as they returned with a basket of eggs. "Can I get that coffee now?"

"Yes, coffee," said Derik, relieved to no longer be alone with John.

Stella nodded. "Have a seat, boys, coming right up."

† † †

CHAPTER 9

John Palmer plodded along the trail to town, his pipe dangling precariously from his mouth. Stella's shopping list wasn't all that long, but most of the morning would be shot by the time he was finished. His thoughts turned to their only boarding guest, who seemed content to sit around and do nothing. Every interaction yielded vague answers, which made John continually suspicious.

The business with Van Sant, his former friend, and Pierce's attempt to kill them all last year left him somewhat paranoid. *Probably all in my head,* he thought.

He pushed the thoughts away, the painful memory of his daughter's death always near the surface. He nudged the horse gently in the ribs, and she broke into a gallop. He kicked her again, pushing her harder as though he could escape his thoughts. She was breathing hard now, yet he didn't let up, the alders lining the trail flying by in a blur.

The horse balked as the coyote burst out of the brush in front of them. They looked at each other for an instant before the coyote loped across the trail and disappeared. The horse snorted and pranced in a half-circle, her coat now glistening with sweat. John patted her neck until she settled, then allowed her to proceed at a leisurely pace.

"Sorry old girl. I shouldn't push you so hard."

The horse snorted and rocked her head up and down as if to agree. *There'd be hell to pay if I rode Stella's horse to death,* he thought as the town came into view.

A thought came to him as he neared the telegraph office, and he stopped, mulling it over. It was a possibility, but Thomas would have to agree. *Only one way to find out.* He dismounted, tied the horse to the rail, and entered the office.

"Good morning," said the clerk. "What can I do for you today, Mr. Palmer?"

"Just a short message," said John as he took the pad from the counter and wrote:

```
THOMAS THORNTON
CHICKEN, ALASKA

HAVE A POTENTIAL BUYER FOR ANGEL
CREEK CLAIM. LET ME KNOW IF YOU
ARE AMENABLE TO SALE.

YOUR DECISION.

JOHN PALMER
VALDEZ, ALASKA
```

"Oh, lucky you stopped in," said the clerk as he rummaged through a stack of messages. "Here—came in a bit ago."

John took the message, glanced at it long enough to see it was from Thomas, and stuffed it in his pocket. He handed the pad to the clerk who counted the words and handed it off to the telegraph operator seated behind him.

"Getting out of the mining business, eh?"

John glared. It was one thing to have them read every message, but inserting themselves into the conversation was another. "Just send it."

John paid the clerk then left, slamming the door on

the way out. He stopped and took a deep breath, angry that he had lost his temper. *Alaska is a big place—why was it so hard to keep things private?* He shook his head and walked across the street to the store.

He wasn't sure how Thomas would react to the telegram. They had never talked about selling Angel Creek, but with two claims, there was no way he and Sdzeè could work both without hiring a crew. Unless something changed, John had no intention of returning to the claim. Selling Angel Creek would allow Thomas to buy out his share and give him some much-needed cash.

John walked across the street to the store. Noel's small store was gone—run out of business by the much larger *A.J. Fish & Co.* The store was bigger—more inventory, variety, and of course, higher prices. He felt sorry for Noel, but that was the price of progress. John entered and went straight to the counter, handing the clerk Stella's list rather than browsing for himself.

"Can you fill that for me, please?"

The clerk nodded, looking at the list. "Shouldn't take me but a few minutes."

John remembered the telegram and pulled it out of his pocket. *News concerning our late nemesis Van Sant?* He shoved the message back into his pocket. It was probably too soon, but perhaps the letter Thomas mentioned was waiting for him.

John headed for the door. "Have to go to the post office—be back directly."

The post office was just down the street—a small wood-frame structure with a lone window. It was painted bright red, a color scheme that seemed odd to John. *Maybe it was used for something else before it was a post office,* he thought as he opened the door.

The interior was simple—a single counter with pigeonhole boxes on the wall behind, and a short wooden bench below the window. A young woman stood behind the counter, pulling letters from an overstuffed mailbag. She didn't look up.

"Hello."

The woman looked up, pushed her spectacles up on her nose, and brushed her curly brown hair from her eyes. "Oh, hello. What can I do for you?"

John had never met her before. "You must be new."

"Yes, just started here this week. Actually, I'm just filling in—the regular fellow is out sick. I'm Rebecca."

"Ah, nice to meet you, Rebecca. Can you see if there's anything for me? John Palmer?"

"I'll try. This just came in from up north, and I haven't even sorted it yet. Mail from the states is coming later in the week on one of the steamers."

"I'm expecting something from Chicken."

She nodded and continued pulling letters from the bag, all the while checking the names. Her hair kept falling over her face, and she kept brushing it away in vain. She let out a puff of air, hoping to get the curls out of the way.

John laughed. "Having a problem?"

She scowled, then grinned. "I guess I need to tie this mop up when I'm working."

"I'm surprised there's so much mail coming from up north," said John.

"All those lonesome miners writing to their ladies back home, I suppose," she said.

"I suppose that could be. Either that or asking for more money to keep on mining."

She smiled at him. "I suppose you've heard the common saying about that."

John shook his head. "Not sure."

"What did the miner say when asked what he would do with a million dollars?"

John thought for a second. "I don't know. What?"

"Mine until it's all gone," said Rebecca, then broke into a shrill laugh.

John chuckled. "That's pretty good—too bad it's close to the truth."

"I know. I could tell you stories. This one time—"

"My letter, please?"

"Oh, sorry. I get carried away with stories. Just wish I could tell which ones were true."

John drummed his fingers gently on the counter. "And there lies the problem."

A handful of letters went flying out of her hand onto the floor in front of John. Rebecca scowled, then blushed. "I'm sorry—feeling a bit rushed."

John stopped drumming, picked up the letters from the floor, and placed them on the counter in front of her. "Don't worry or hurry on my account."

"Thank you." She picked up one of the letters, then laughed. "This one is for you," she said, extending her hand.

John took the letter—it was from Chicken. "This is just what I was looking for."

Rebecca nodded and continued with her sorting task. "It'll be a few more minutes before I get through the rest of this. You can have a seat and wait in case there's something else for you."

"I'm not expecting anything else, but I'll wait." John sat down on the bench, then opened the letter:

```
Dear John,

I hesitate to write regarding this subject
but thought you should know.  An odd incident
took place.  Someone dug up Van Sant's grave
and stole his clothes.  We found them later all
ripped up, but a slip of paper was found in
the lining of the coat.  Most curious, it read:

"Your Destiny lies on the NP befour you leave."

I have no idea what this means, but perhaps
the grave robber was searching for it.  I
further investigated and found what was left
of his belongings at the post office.  Nothing
of interest was found but a slip of paper with
this:

DH&C 6836

Maybe all this means something, or perhaps it's
nothing.  I thought you should know and didn't
want it exposed to prying eyes via telegram.

Best,

Thomas
```

John stared at the cryptic phrase, wracking his brain for what it could mean. At the moment, it meant absolutely nothing. He folded the letter and put it in his pocket. It was clear what the number *6836* meant. It was his bank account number at Dexter Horton and Company in Seattle—the number Van Sant used to steal the money. John rubbed his forehead. *What in the world is going on?*

† † †

John led the horse into the barn and removed the saddle and bags. He brushed her down quickly, then gave her a bucket of oats. Stella didn't hear him return, apparently busy somewhere in the boarding house. The trip back was a blur, his thoughts consumed with the letter from Thomas. The more he thought about it, the more obscure it seemed. He shook off the feeling, gathered up the supplies, and headed for the back door.

"Here you go," he said as he placed the supplies on the counter.

Stella was busy washing dishes. "Did you get everything?"

"I think so—maybe."

Stella stopped and looked at him. "Maybe?"

"I'm sorry. I'm a bit distracted. While in town, I got a telegram from Thomas saying he sent a letter about Van Sant.

"Oh?"

"Yes, so I went to the post office and fetched it. It's very odd."

"What did it say?"

John pulled the letter from his pocket and handed it to Stella. She read through it, looked up at John, then reread it.

"This is very strange. What does it all mean?"

"Obviously, it has something to do with the money—or at least it seems so. That's the bank account number, but I have no idea what the note found on Van Sant's clothes means."

The chair in the dining room made a scraping sound as it was pushed away from the table. John, eyes wide, looked at Stella, then whispered, "Is *he* in the dining room?"

Stella nodded. John cursed under his breath. This was nobody's business but theirs.

"Do you think he heard us?"

Stella nodded. "Most likely."

"Blast it."

John took the letter from Stella and stuffed it in his pocket. "Let's put these supplies away," he said loudly, just as Derik appeared in the kitchen doorway.

"Anything I can help with?" said Derik, his eyes scanning the room.

"No, we've got it covered," said John.

Derik continued to gaze around the room.

"Looking for something?" said John.

"Oh, no. Guess I'll head outside for a smoke."

"You do that."

Derik half grinned, turned, and left. John wasn't sure if it was a grin or a sneer. "I don't like that man. He's too interested in our affairs."

Stella nodded. "Maybe it's just his personality. Some people are naturally nosy, you know."

"Don't care. He needs to move on. I think I'll ask him to leave. He can stay at the *Valdez House.*

"Don't be rash, John. You're probably reading too much into it."

John sighed. "Maybe. I wish Thomas was here so I could talk with him. This back and forth by telegram or letter is so difficult."

"I know, dear."

"Well, I guess he can stay for now, but we need to be more careful when he's around."

Stella nodded, then grinned. "Now help me put these groceries away, or you'll get no dinner."

Derik sat on the bench in the corner of the porch, his feet up on the rail. He drew a long drag on his cigarette, all the while keeping an ear open. He'd missed much of what was said by the two in the kitchen, but two things he heard clearly—*bank account* and *Van Sant.*

He wasn't sure what it meant, but it had to be one of two things. Either they had the money or knew where it was. The letter must have the answer. *I have to get my hands on that letter.*

It wouldn't be easy. If only there was a way to get them both out of the house for a while. From what he'd seen, Stella didn't leave, being too consumed with keeping things up around the place, but there might be a way to lure her to town.

Another nighttime search of the place was risky, especially since he didn't know where the letter might be hiding. Odds were it would be close to John, either on him or perhaps in their room at night. If they had the money, it probably wasn't at the boarding house. Maybe that bank account was the key. He was closer—he could taste it. All that remained was to work out the details. Derik smiled and took another drag. *No small task.*

CHAPTER 10

Derik finished up the last bite of eggs and took a huge gulp of coffee. "Stella, this was a magnificent breakfast."

"Why, thank you, Derik. Just simple frontier fare."

"Well, it certainly hit the spot. By the way, where's John?"

"He's out tending to morning chores—feeding the chickens, putting the horse out to graze, and so forth."

"Ah," said Derik. "Say, you folks have been great hosts. I'd really like to do something for you."

"That's not necessary. After all, you're paying for it," said Stella.

"I know, but you two deserve a night out, and since I'm the only guest, I'd like to treat you to dinner tonight in town—at Wikidel's."

"Wikidel's? That's the most expensive place in town."

"Well, they do bill themselves as the most elegant restaurant in the Northwest."

"We really couldn't accept. It's too much."

Come, come Stella. I really want to do this."

"Well, I'll talk to John about it."

"I have to go to town this afternoon to run some errands and send a telegram, so I could meet you there at around six this evening."

"I've never been there but have heard good things about it," said Stella.

"Well, all the more reason to go. It's settled then—I'll meet you two there tonight and won't take no for an answer. My treat."

Stella smiled. "Okay, I'll twist John's arm if I have to."

Derik stood, handed his plate to Stella, then turned away, a broad grin spreading across his face.

† † †

Derik sat on the edge of a small clearing on a hill about a quarter-mile from Stella's boarding house. After ensuring John was on board with his dinner invitation, he had left to do his nonexistent errands in town. Now he sat, smoking a cigarette and watching.

The boarding house was in clear view, and with his horse tied off in the nearby brush, he was confident no one would notice him—especially the Palmers. All he had to do was wait until they left, then he could get about his business. With the travel time to and from town, he figured they would be gone at least an hour. If they stayed for dinner despite his absence, even longer. If all went well, he'd have time to search and still show up before they became suspicious.

Derik crushed out his third cigarette and stared across the valley to the boarding house. He looked at his pocket watch and sighed. Still no sign of them. *Maybe they changed their mind.*

He sat there long enough for the spring crop of hungry mosquitoes to find him, continually dive-bombing him as he swatted the air. Several had already snuck in under his collar to feast on his neck before being crushed into a bloody smear. In desperation, he rolled another cigarette and lit up, puffing furiously to create a cloud of smoke. It helped—though not entirely—the pests still buzzed about him. It didn't help that he was sitting near a swampy area, despite being on the side of a hill. It seemed you could find soggy ground nearly anywhere in Alaska, even on the side of a mountain, and with it, an abundance of bugs.

The horse was thrashing around behind him, a cloud of bugs harassing her as well. *This is great,* he thought as he lit up yet another cigarette. He looked at his watch again, all the while praying for a breeze to provide relief from the mosquitoes. He was just about to give it up when he spotted Palmer's horse and wagon appear from behind the boarding house. He strained to see and was finally able to tell—both John and Stella were on board.

Derik watched as they moved out of sight, around a bend in the trail. He jumped up, untied the horse, and mounted up. The urge to rush down there—to get away from the horde of bugs—was overwhelming, but he forced himself to wait. The last thing he needed was to ride down there only to have them come back if they forgot something. It wasn't likely, but he had to be careful. He waited five minutes and decided to risk it. He slapped the reins across the horse's rump, and she took off on a dead run, happy it seemed to get off the hill.

From his hiding spot, it only took a few minutes to reach the trail. He stopped and listened for the sound of the wagon, the distinctive creaking of the wheels always a dead giveaway. Hearing nothing, he pressed on to the boarding house, deciding to tie the horse up around back in the event someone happened by. It wouldn't do for anyone to notice his presence. He made his way around the rear of the house, past the barn, and to the back door.

He paused, realizing if it was locked, his plan of stealth would be in jeopardy. He slowly turned the knob and pushed. The door swung open with ease.

Where to search first? The door to the small office was closed. He opened it and thought about searching the desk, but it would take some time with the number of papers. No—searching upstairs, a place he hadn't been, would be first. He made his way up the creaking stairs and down the hall to their bedroom. He'd never been in that room—no legitimate reason to do so thus far.

The door was closed—and locked. He cursed under his breath, stared for a moment, then returned downstairs to the office. The rolltop desk was closed. Derik noticed it had a small, brass-colored lock, apparently for securing it from prying eyes. He grasped the wooden handles on each side and gently pulled upward, hoping it was free. He breathed a sigh of relief as the top smoothly rolled up.

Surely the letter was here somewhere. He shuffled quickly through the invoices, receipts, and other mundane artifacts of running the boarding house. The nooks at the back of the desk held even more paperwork, neatly organized by category. Derik's eyes brightened as he pulled the stack from the upper left compartment and realized they were personal letters.

Now we're getting somewhere, he thought as he quickly began shuffling through each one. From the overheard conversation, he remembered the letter was from a Thomas, who he assumed was Thornton. He recognized none of the names on the return addresses. He finished looking through them, cursed, and shoved the stack unceremoniously back into the nook on the bottom left. *It's not here.*

He turned his attention to the drawers but found nothing of interest—no letter and no clues as to where the money was hidden—if they even had it. He looked at his watch and sighed loudly. Already a half-hour was gone. Palmer would be at the restaurant soon. He had to move quickly, but breaking down the door to their bedroom would expose his intentions. He sat down at the desk. *Think—think.* He shoved away from the desk—then saw it. Hanging from a small hook at the back of a compartment was a key—a key that looked like it would unlock the door he so badly needed open.

† † †

John looked at his pocket watch for the third time in ten minutes. "Humph. Where is he?"

Stella ceased her gazing at Wikidel's furnishings and looked at John. "I don't know. What time is it?"

"It's 6:20 and no sign of him. Weren't we supposed to meet Derik at six?"

"Yes. Maybe he got tied up. He said he had a bunch of errands to do or some such."

John frowned. "Well, he better show up soon."

Stella took his hands in hers and smiled. "Or what? You're leaving?"

John's look softened and returned the smile. "No, I guess we'll have a date night. Just the two of us."

"That'd be nice."

"Wonder what this place costs."

"I'm sure it's not too bad. We can afford it if our host skips on us."

John nodded. "It's quite fancy though, what with these cozy little round tables and white linen tablecloths."

"And folded napkins too," said Stella. "Look, I have two spoons and two forks."

"That's how you can tell how much the meal is going to cost. Just count the number of utensils and multiply by ten or more."

Stella laughed. "Oh John, you're quite funny at times."

The waiter arrived with a pitcher of water and refilled their glasses. "Can I get you something else to drink?"

"No, we'll stick with water for now."

The waiter nodded. "We have an excellent red wine for you this evening if you're interested. Just arrived on the boat today."

John waved his hand.

"Very good, sir. Are you ready to order?"

"No, we're still expecting one more. We'll wait a bit longer."

The waiter nodded and retreated.

"Did you see how fancy he was dressed?" said Stella.

"Didn't notice."

Stella shook her head. "You better shape up, mister, or there'll be no breakfast for you tomorrow."

John frowned, then smiled. "Okay. I'm just a bit aggravated that he invites us here and doesn't show. I can't help wonder where he is."

† † †

Derik pushed the horse harder, her nostrils flaring and mane flying as the trail flew by. He whipped her again with the reins. "Faster, you worthless nag."

The search of the bedroom took longer than expected. It would have gone faster if he could have just tossed the place, but it was too soon to reveal his hand. Pleased with himself after finding the key, his mood quickly changed as the search progressed. Drawers, a vanity, even the mattress yielded nothing—no letter—no hint of the money.

He had made sure everything was just as he found it, then hurried. It was after six—he was late, and with each minute, he feared that John would grow suspicious. It was clear Palmer didn't like him—it wouldn't take much to put everything in jeopardy. His worst fear was meeting the Palmers on the trail. If they caught him headed into town, it would be tough to explain.

As the horse galloped on, his mind raced. *What next?* Further searching seemed futile. He had to come up with a plan and had to do it quickly. The town came into view, and he slowed the horse to a trot, then pulled out his pocket watch. He cursed at the time—6:35 p.m. He was accustomed to being quick with a lie but struggled to come up with an explanation for being tardy.

Wikidel's came into view, and he was relieved to see Palmer's horse and wagon out front. He reached the restaurant and tied off the horse—now sporting a thick lather from the ride. If Palmer saw it, he'd wonder why the horse was so worked up—nothing he could do about it. He quickly brushed the dust from his pants, took a deep breath, and entered.

It took a minute for his eyes to adjust to the darkened interior. He scanned the spacious room, filled with tables and diners, finally spotting them. He headed directly for the table, not waiting to be seated.

"Whew—made it. Sorry, I'm so late. I'm glad you're still here."

John looked up, eyes narrowed. "We were just about to leave."

"I'm glad you didn't," said Derik as he pulled out a chair and sat down across from them.

"Why are you so late?"

"Had some trouble at the outfitters. I got a telegram from my partner regarding some things we needed, and I lost track of time. I'm sorry."

John scanned his face, looking for a tell. "I thought you said your partner had that all taken care of."

Derik forced a laugh. "Well, I thought so too. But, you know how things go."

John crossed his arms. "When's he getting here?"

Derik shifted in his chair. "Uh...not sure. He had some problems back home, so it's delayed his departure." The excuse for his nonexistent partner wasn't much, but maybe enough.

"That's unfortunate," said John, his arms still crossed.

The waiter approached the table, then filled Derik's water glass. "Ready to order now?"

Derik nodded. "Yes, and you folks order whatever you want—it's on me."

"Thank you, Derik," said Stella.

The waiter took the orders and turned to leave. Derik grabbed his arm, startling him. "Yes?"

"Bring me a whiskey—no, make it two."

"Yes, sir. You folks want anything else to drink?"

Stella shook her head. "No, we're fine," said John.

An odd silence settled over the table. Derik tried to come up with a line of questioning that wouldn't raise suspicion, but he was still frazzled from the hurried search and thundering ride in.

"So, what are your plans now that your partner is delayed," said Stella, finally breaking the silence.

"Not sure. I might pack up and head north. You know—sort of get a jump on things, so to speak."

John folded his hands. "So you'll be leaving us soon then."

Derik nodded. "Probably in a day or two."

"Well, that's good. Good to get a jump on things," said John.

The waiter brought the whiskey, then returned with the food. Small talk ensued, with Derik telling stories about things that never happened.

John grew tired of it all and finished his meal quickly, hoping to draw an end to the evening. He looked at Stella, sitting there listening intently to Derik. *She's a better person than I am*, thought John. After another fifteen minutes of one-sided conversation, he motioned for the waiter.

"Can we have the check, please?"

The waiter nodded and retreated.

"You ready to leave already?" said Derik. "It's still early—I thought we could make an evening of it."

John shot Stella a glance, which was immediately interpreted. "No, I don't care for the trip back in the dark, so we need to get going."

Derik gulped the last shot of whiskey. "Sorry to hear that."

The waiter returned and offered the check to John, who in turn pointed at Derik. "I believe you said this was your treat?"

"Right," said Derik as he rummaged through first his vest pocket, then all the others. "Blast it."

"What's wrong?" said Stella.

"Seems I've left my wallet back at your place."

John shook his head, then snatched the check from Derik. "Come, Stella, let's head for home."

Stella nodded, and they both stood. John turned to Derik. "I'd say thanks for the meal, but of course, it didn't turn out that way."

Stella cringed a bit and took his arm, turning John

toward the door.

"I'm very sorry. I'll pay you back," said Derik.

John ignored him, moved to the door, and paid the bill. Derik watched them leave, then motioned for the waiter. "I'll have another whiskey," he said, pulling a couple of bills from his wallet and placing them on the table.

CHAPTER 11

Stella set a steaming cup of black coffee in front of John, then sat down across from him at the dining room table. She glanced at the stairs leading to the guest rooms. Sunrise was barely a glimmer, the sun readying an appearance.

"You think he's still asleep?" said Stella.

John glanced at his watch. "It's only a little after five. My bet is yes."

"Quite the dinner last night," said Stella.

John took a swig of coffee, then shook his head. "Yeah, probably never see that money. Invites us to the most expensive place in Valdez, then stiffs us on the bill."

"I'm sure it was an honest mistake."

"You're too trusting, Stella. There's something wrong with that fellow."

"Like what?"

"Like his vague answer to almost every question."

"You might be right. Shall we ask him to leave?"

"Maybe. We've had dodgy guests before, but I get a bad feeling about this one."

Stella took a sip of coffee. "He may not like being asked to leave."

"Don't care. This is your place."

"Our place, but we don't want to get a bad reputation for kicking out our guests."

"One won't hurt."

"Maybe we should wait."

"For what?"

"Let's see his reaction today—especially if he pays for last night's dinner," said Stella.

John nodded, then pushed back his chair and stood. "I'm going to take care of morning chores. Let me know when breakfast is ready."

"I'll need some firewood when you get a chance. The wood box is empty."

"You got it," said John as he headed through the kitchen to the back door.

Stella went to the kitchen and held her hand over the big cast-iron cooking stove. A bit of warmth met her. *Good, at least there's some coals left.* She pulled the skillet from its hook and placed it on the stove, then set about collecting ingredients for John's breakfast. Five minutes later, he returned with an armful of wood.

"Just in time," said Stella.

John reached the firebox, then stumbled against the box, dropping half the wood. The box scraped across the floor and away from the wall by a couple of inches. His jaw dropped.

"Look," he said as he moved the box out of the way and pointed.

Stella gasped. The small hatch that concealed their hiding place was ajar. "Maybe it just popped open when you tripped."

John pried the hatch open. The jars were gone. "Well, that tears it. We've been robbed."

"John, that was nearly everything we have," said Stella,

tears welling up in her eyes.

"I know. And I can tell you who the number one suspect is."

"Do you think?"

"It would explain why he was late to dinner."

"What shall we do?"

"Go ahead with breakfast. When he comes down, we'll set this straight," said John. He replaced the hatch, put the firewood in the box, and slid it back against the wall. He turned and looked at Stella, the vein on his forehead bulging. "This won't be pretty."

† † †

"Good morning," said Derik as he sat down at the table. "How are you today, Stella?"

Stella brought him a cup of coffee from the kitchen. "Fine."

Derik grabbed the cup, held it in both hands, then took a sip. "Good coffee, ma'am, but some cream would make it brilliant."

Stella shrugged her shoulders. "Sorry, we haven't had a cow around here since before my first husband died."

"Ah," said Derik, taking another sip.

"Breakfast will be ready in just a couple minutes."

"Take your time," said Derik.

The back door opened, and John entered the kitchen. He removed two items from the top shelf above the stove, then headed for the dining room.

"Mornin', John," said Derik.

John said nothing as he reached the table and placed two empty Mason jars in front of Derik, a mere inch from his coffee cup. John sat down, leaned back in his chair, and put his arms behind his head. Derik stared blankly at the jars.

"What's this?"

John just stared at him. Derik shifted his weight in his chair, then lifted his cup. John thought he saw a slight tremor as Derik took a gulp, but he wasn't sure. Derik looked at him, waiting.

"Those look familiar to you?"

"Uh, well, I think everyone has seen a Mason jar."

"Seen any others around here?"

Derik shrugged, then stared into his coffee cup. "Not really."

"Well, we have a problem," said John.

"I don't know what you're talking about."

"I think you do."

Derik shook his head. "No, sir, I do not."

"Why were you late to dinner last night?"

"I told you already. Got tied up at the outfitters."

"Strange," said John. "I thought they closed before six."

Derik took a sip, then nearly knocked his cup over trying to set it down. "Well, they stayed open since I was already there."

"I see," said John. "Here's what I think happened. I think you weren't at the outfitters at all. I think you were here, going through our things when you happened upon two mason jars—one with cash and the other with gold dust and nuggets."

Derik cleared his throat. "That's crazy. I told you where I was."

"I don't believe you."

"That's your problem—I'm telling the truth."

"Prove it," said John, now leaning forward, fists clasped on the table.

"How?"

"Let me search your room."

Derik laughed. "If it will make you happy, go ahead."

John stood up from the table—Derik started to do the same.

"No. You stay here."

"I will not."

John slammed his fists on the table. "You will, or else."

Derik clenched his teeth, but said nothing, then sank back down in his chair.

Stella entered the dining room and set a plate in front of Derik, then retreated silently to the kitchen. Derik watched as John ascended the stairs. A thin smile spread slowly across his face.

John returned a few minutes later with Derik's bag in hand and dropped it unceremoniously on the floor by the front door. Derik looked at him.

"Well? Didn't find anything, did you," said Derik.

"No, but you're out of here, just as soon as I search your saddlebags."

"Fine," said Derik. "Can I at least finish my breakfast?"

John ignored him and left through the back door, headed for the barn. He was gone for longer than Derik expected. Shortly he returned with nothing in his hands.

"I told you," said Derik. "I have no idea what you're talking about."

"I want you out now," said John as he brushed past

Stella. "I saddled your horse."

Derik stood, held his fork two feet above the plate, then dropped it. "Gladly."

"You owe us for the time here, and dinner at Wikidels."

Derik laughed. "If you think I'm paying you anything after the way I've been treated, you're daft."

John stepped forward quickly, but Stella hooked his arm, then spoke calmly. "John, no. Let's cut our losses and let him go."

John grunted. "This isn't over, Tannvas."

Derik said nothing, picked up his bag, and opened the door. He paused and turned back to look at John. "You're right about that."

The door slammed shut, and he was gone. John looked out the window and watched as Derik stowed his bag on the horse, then mounted up and rode away, headed toward town.

"I know he stole our money," said John finally.

Stella nodded. "Possibly, but it's not here."

"Now we're really in a bind."

"We will be okay," said Stella. "We have some money at the bank, and I'm sure we'll be getting some gold from Thomas this season."

John shook his head, then slumped in a chair. "I suppose. But I wonder if I shouldn't go north and help him work the claims since we're near poverty now."

"Let's hold off. I really don't want you to leave me alone."

"We could close up. Go north again."

"You weren't happy there, especially after what happened with Emily."

John knew she was right. Working the claim every day where his daughter was shot and killed wasn't something he wanted to endure. The nightmares were still strong and frequent. Returning to the scene could only make it worse.

"Right," said John. "I'll head into the town, get some cash and check the bank balance, then send a telegram to Thomas."

"Sounds fine," said Stella. "But please wait until tomorrow. I want to be sure he's not coming back. Breakfast is ready, and the bank will still be there tomorrow."

John nodded. *She's right, as usual.*

Derik turned off the trail a mile from the boarding house and nudged the horse through a thick stand of alders. He continued onward, the alders opening up into a meadow of tall grass and few trees, with a game trail running through the middle. He stopped and listened, then continued on another hundred yards to a mixed stand of spruce and cottonwood. He stopped, dismounted, and tied off the horse, then proceeded to the base of a large cottonwood. Pulling back a loose clump of moss revealed what he was after—two Mason jars.

Derik smiled. Palmer would never know—at least never be able to prove—that he took them. He could sell the gold in Valdez but had to be careful. Though the town had grown in the last five years, it was still a small community, rife with gossip. He placed the jars in the saddlebag, then mounted up, pointing the horseback to the trail. He paused before entering the alder stand, wanting to ensure no one was coming. Satisfied, he pushed through and pointed the horse toward town.

He found the jars quite by accident, tripping over the wood box while searching the boarding house. He noticed the little hatch, pried it open, and discovered the two jars. It was a small reward compared to his goal, but if all else failed, at least the trip wouldn't be a total waste.

He didn't push the horse—there was no hurry to get to Valdez. Besides, it gave him time to think—time to plan what to do next. Searching yielded nothing. It seemed the only way to get the answers he needed was to trick or force Palmer into revealing them. As the miles passed, he failed to come up with anything clever. One thing was pretty clear, Palmer hated him—he wouldn't reveal anything voluntarily.

A plan slowly came to mind, but it was one of last resort. Once put into motion, it was the final play. What he had in mind meant one thing—once it was over, whether successful or not, he'd need to be on the next boat south.

CHAPTER 12

John reached the telegraph office just before noon. With Derik gone, he'd spent the day before inventorying the house and barn while Stella checked the office and remainder of the boarding house. They'd found nothing else missing—nothing out of place. John thought about every interaction with their wayward guest—how it always seemed off in some way. He wasn't a particularly suspicious person, but if the events of the last year taught him anything, it was to be careful—not to trust too quickly.

Derik seemed overly interested in their business, and though he wasn't sure, John thought he'd met him before. The name, *Tannvas* wasn't familiar to him, but yet something about him was familiar. Stella was sure she'd never seen him before. *Maybe I'm paranoid.*

In any event, he decided to send John a telegram, acknowledging receipt of the letter and warning him about Tannvas. He knew he was headed to the Interior, assuming any of his vague answers had even an element of truth.

Before he reached the counter of the telegraph office, the clerk held out the message pad and pencil. John nodded, and the clerk placed them on the counter.

"Just sending one today," said John. "Do you have

anything for me?"

"Pretty sure not, but I'll take a look," said the clerk.

John nodded again and wrote:

```
THOMAS THORNTON
CHICKEN, ALASKA

RECEIVED LETTER. NO IDEA OF
MEANING YET. SUSPICIOUS DEALING
WITH MAN NAMED DERIK TANNVAS WHO
IS HEADED TO INTERIOR. JUST BEWARE
IF YOU HAPPEN TO MEET.

JOHN PALMER
VALDEZ, ALASKA
```

John handed the pad to the clerk who counted up the words. He waited for some comment about the content of the message, but for once, it didn't happen.

John paid for the message and headed for the door.

"We'll get this out directly," said the clerk.

John nodded and closed the door behind him. As he mounted up, he realized that the message would probably cause Thomas to have a lot of questions. *Maybe I should explain it all in a letter.*

He rode down the street to the *Gold Dust Exchange*, one of the few places in town to sell raw gold. Most places wouldn't buy it without an assay, but Al White, the proprietor, would. *It's worth a shot,* he thought as he wrapped the reins around the hitching rail, patted the horse on the neck, and entered the building.

The office was devoid of customers, except for a grizzled old man sleeping in the only chair in the corner. The walls were decorated with many framed, yellowing newspaper clippings about the gold rush. The air was stale with the smell of cigarettes and old miners—something that gave the place an ambiance of its own.

John approached the counter and rang the bell next to a large set of gold scales. A man appeared from the back room. John didn't recognize him—it wasn't Al.

"Looking to sell some gold?"

John shook his head. "Not this time. I'm looking for some information."

"Oh?"

"Yes. I was wondering if anyone has come in lately to sell gold dust in a Mason jar."

The man laughed. "No, not that I recall—why?"

"I'm just looking for someone. Have you been working here the last couple of days?"

"Yeah, but business has been kind of slow. We bought a large quantity of gold from a miner just in from the Chisana district. Real nice, coarse gold."

"That wouldn't be who I'm looking for. This was pretty fine gold with a few nuggets—all from the Fortymile."

"Nope. Nothing like that in the last day or two."

John turned to leave. "Thanks. I might check back with you again. If someone does come in with a jar full of gold, try to find out where they're staying."

The man rubbed his chin. "Not sure I want to do that, friend. Our customers value their privacy."

"I'll make it worthwhile."

"You can check back. I'll decide if I'm going to help when the time comes."

"Thanks," said John as he left.

That's probably a dead end. Derik would have to be pretty stupid to try and sell the gold while still in the jar. He wasn't one hundred percent sure Derik was the thief, but the odds were good. For all John knew, he may have already moved on. Any hope of recovering the money and gold was quickly fading.

He thought about checking with the hotels to see if Derik was still in town but decided it would be pointless. He wasn't about to sit outside a hotel to see if he could catch him doing something incriminating.

After a brief stop at the bank and store, John nudged the horse homeward, his thoughts wandering over his life since coming to Alaska. He'd lost much—a wife, a daughter, a fortune, and now their savings. The one bright spot was Stella—she was the spark that kept him going.

The spring day was warm—the fragrance of budding leaves filled the air as the horse plodded along. His mind wandered, filled with images of days gone by. Along the isolated stretch of trail, he stopped, filled his pipe, and lit up. As he nudged the horse forward, a sudden noise from the brush to his right startled him. The horse turned wildly as John struggled to hold on.

"What are you doing here, you—"

† † †

Stella looked at the pocket watch, then replaced it on the shelf. It was past dinner time, and John wasn't home. Several times the sound of a horse reached her ears, only to be yet another traveler passing by on the trail. Dinner was cold, but that didn't concern her. The sun wouldn't set for at least another hour—she was thankful the days had grown longer in the north, especially today. *What will I do if he's not home by dark?* she thought as she stared out the front window. A gnawing feeling settled in her stomach. She fought back the thoughts—the memories of the day her first husband didn't come home.

The evening wore on, and she became more anxious with each passing hour. Stella paced between the kitchen and dining room, stopping to stare out the window with each lap. Finally, she fetched the lantern from the kitchen, lit it, and hung it on a hook above the railing of the porch. She went inside and returned with a blanket, then sat on the bench, and covered up. She pulled the blanket up around her neck and stared down the trail. The blanket provided little comfort—Stella found herself shaking as she played the scenarios over in her mind.

I'm probably worried for nothing—most likely, he's all right.

CHAPTER 13

Stella dropped the hot cup of coffee and watched as it shattered across the floor. She pressed her shaking hands against her side, trying in vain to still them. Sleep evaded her—she spent the night in the living room, staring out the window into the dark, waiting for John.

As she cleaned up the glass, her thoughts raced back and forth—from wondering where John was, to what happened to her first husband. Wesley met a horrifying end in an encounter with a bear, and just as bad, she hadn't known what happened for five years until Thomas finally found his remains high in the mountains.

John was only headed to town and back. She racked her brain for an explanation, but none came. The need to find him—the need to get to town overwhelmed her. John had the only horse—it meant she faced a long walk. She took Wesley's pocket watch from the mantle and looked at it yet again. Nearly six—the first hints of sunrise would peek over the mountains soon. She readied herself for the walk, hands still trembling. *I can't go through this again.*

She bundled up and stepped out on the porch. The cold spring air hit her in the face. Until the sun came up, it would be cold—she braced herself for it, descended the stairs, and started out. Walking briskly, she quickly warmed up, so much so she had to unbutton her coat. She stepped into a wagon rut and nearly turned her ankle. *I need to slow down.*

After a mile, it was fully light, allowing her to pick up the pace without fear of stumbling in the dark. The trail was a mix of terrain, from gravel bars near the river, to open meadows and thick tunnels of alder. She hurried through the alder-lined areas, the lack of visibility adding to her already frayed nerves.

As she entered a long stretch of alder, a sudden sound to her left made her freeze in her tracks. In her hurry to get underway, she didn't think to bring a rifle. Though unlikely, the chance of a bear encounter was always a possibility. The noise rapidly approached—she peered into the alders while slowly backing away. It burst out into the middle of the trail and stopped—a snowshoe hare, its fur coat halfway between winter white and summer brown. Pausing only a second, it hopped quickly into the alders on the other side. Stella breathed out deeply, then laughed out loud. *Get a hold of yourself, woman.*

It was at least a two-hour walk to town, and Stella realized she would be arriving before many of the establishments were open. No matter—hopefully, the telegraph office and store would be open. She'd stop there first, then check at the bank to determine when John was last seen. Her thoughts kept up their nagging pace, despite her attempts to think positive. Surely there was a simple explanation—the horse became lame, or John fell ill—any number of things better than the worse scenario her mind conjured up.

She hurried on, hoping someone would come along and offer her a ride. That was unlikely since it was quite early, and anyone leaving from a roadhouse up the trail would still be hours away. She stopped for only a minute or two to catch her breath. Not moving, the cold caught up with her, and she started shivering. *Or is it nerves?* She pulled the coat tight around her and pressed on.

† † †

Thomas read the telegram, shook his head, and reread it. The message from John about Derik Tannvas was perplexing. *What did John mean by "suspicious dealings"?* Thomas stuffed the telegram in his pocket, nodded at the clerk, and left the telegraph office. *I wish I could just talk to John,* he thought as he untied the horse and mounted up.

The horse plodded along, headed back to the mining claim. Thomas didn't push her, being lost in thought. They never knew the name of the grave robber—in fact, only a couple of folks got a good look at him. The alias he used was dull-witted—*A. Friend.* That wasn't going to fool anyone. A few moments later, Thomas reigned in the horse, then rolled a cigarette. He stared out across the valley, snow still capping the higher rolling hills of the Fortymile country. He took a long drag. *Maybe that truly was his name.* It didn't much matter—there was no way to trace him since he left town. Thomas decided a description of this Tannvas fellow was needed. With that, he could ask around and see if it matched that of A. Friend.

Thomas stopped and took stock of his surroundings. He wasn't sure how far he'd traveled while lost in thought. *Still on the main trail.* That meant he wasn't more than a mile or so out of Chicken. He turned the horse around and kicked her gently in the ribs. She lurched forward, settling into a steady gallop. The only way to get a description of Tannvas was to get it from John, and a letter from him was the best way. He hurried on, intent on sending a telegram that would hopefully result in a letter to solve the mystery of the grave robber.

Stella was walking much slower when Valdez came into view. She pushed too hard at the beginning and was now tired. She couldn't tell if the knot in her stomach was from worry or hunger. Food would have to wait. She looked at Wesley's pocket watch. *Nearly nine.* The telegraph office and store would be open. As she neared, it was clear the town was bustling with activity. The spring flood of tenderfoot city-slickers with dreams of getting rich on the goldfields already swelled through the town.

She hurried past the wagons loaded with mining gear and the newly arrived, wide-eyed neophytes surging through the town after arriving on the morning steamer. John likely wouldn't be among them, and her single-minded goal was to reach the telegraph office. She was sure he stopped there.

"Yes, he was here yesterday," said the telegraph clerk. "Sent a message to someone and then left."

"Did he say where he was going?" said Stella.

"Nope, and I didn't see which way he went."

Stella nodded, thanked the clerk, and stepped outside. She wasn't sure where to go next. John mentioned the telegraph office and the bank for sure. Beyond that, maybe the store. She headed up the street in that direction, her legs now aching from the march to town. She passed the bank—it was still closed. Arriving at *A.J. Fish & Co.* she entered and paused, waiting for her eyes to adjust to the light.

"May I help you?" said the young woman behind the counter.

"Yes, I hope so. Do you know my husband, John Palmer?"

She shook her head. "Don't think I do."

"I'm looking for him and wanted to find out if he was in here yesterday. Is there anyone else I could ask?"

"Sorry. I'm the only one here this morning."

Stella stared for a moment, not looking at anything in particular.

"Are you all right, ma'am?"

Stella's eyes focused. "Uh...yes. I'm fine. Thank you."

She brushed past another customer and opened the door to find a towering figure blocking her way. It was Al White.

"Stella. How are you? I heard John was in the shop yesterday, but I missed him."

"He was at the Gold Dust Exchange?"

"Yes, I guess he didn't mention it."

Stella slumped, and tears started to flow.

"My dear, whatever is wrong?"

She struggled with the words. "He didn't come home last night. I've been looking for him."

Al took her hand and guided her to a bench just outside the store. "Here, sit. Now tell me what is going on."

"I don't know anything other than he didn't make it home from town. I didn't see anything of him on my way in." '

"My employee told me he was asking about someone trying to sell gold in Mason jars."

"Oh, that makes sense. We were robbed."

"That's terrible—I'm so sorry."

"I don't care about that now. I just need to find John."

Al nodded, the intimation clear. He'd known Stella and her first husband a long time. "I'm sure he's fine—likely nothing to worry about."

"Was there?" said Stella.

"Sorry?"

"Oh. Was there anyone trying to sell our gold?"

"No, but I told all the employees to keep an eye out."

"Thank you for that." She stood, smoothed her dress, and wiped a tear from her cheek. "I need to keep looking."

"How did you get to town?"

"I walked."

"My word. Come on, let's get over to Jack's and see if he can help you get around."

"I don't want to bother him."

"Nonsense. Besides, he owes me a favor or two."

† † †

The sign above the tiny log cabin read:

JACK'S FREIGHT AND DRAYING

Stella reached for the handle, a twisted chunk of diamond willow nailed to the door, then looked back. "Thank you, Al. I'm sure Jack will help me."

"You're welcome. If he gives you any trouble, let me know."

Stella managed a feeble laugh, then entered the tiny cabin. It was empty, but on the small table in the middle of the room was a slip of paper with a handwritten note:

At the docks. Back after noon.

Stella sighed. With the influx of wannabe miners, a lot of freight and people needed shuttling around town. No wonder Jack was busy. She sat down at the table and looked at the watch. *A little before ten.* The bank would be open soon—she could check there and then wander down to the docks to find Jack, though she wasn't sure what he could do to help other than drive her around. Maybe he'd seen John in his travels yesterday.

The *Bank of Valdez* was small, but since it was the only one in town, its business was thriving. The tellers and manager knew Stella by name—a fact she hoped would aid in finding out where John may have gone. She was wrong.

"He was here, withdrew a small amount of cash, and left," said one of the tellers. "Didn't say where he was going next."

Another dead end. "Thanks," said Stella.

She left the bank and headed toward the docks. Twice she saw a tall man in a hat that caused her to do a double-take. Neither turned out to be John, but that didn't stop her from taking a hard look in the crowds. She couldn't think of why John would spend the night in town—well, there was one. She tried to put it out of her mind.

Rather than wait around, she decided to check with the hotels just in case. There were numerous places to stay in Valdez—one or two could pass for a hotel, the others were more in the style of a communal bunkhouse. After inquiring at nearly all the hotels, including the *Northern* and *St. Elias*, she was satisfied that John didn't spend the night at any of them—no one saw him, and he wasn't on any of the guest registers. The few she didn't check were nothing more than flophouses—a place John would never stay.

The gnawing in her stomach was either hunger or

anxiety—she wasn't sure which. She considered stopping at the cafe for something to eat, then decided her mission was more important. *I'll eat later.* She trudged up the street, aimed for the docks in hopes of finding Jack and that he might have seen John.

The *Olympia* was docked, black smoke belching from her twin stacks. A large throng of passengers stood about, having disembarked and impatiently waiting for both luggage and freight to be unloaded and sorted. A group of wagons lined the street, waiting. Stella walked down the line, looking for Jack. At last, she spotted him, his wagon parked at the very end. He was sitting on the wagon, feet propped up and hat pulled low. It looked like he was asleep—how that was possible among the noise and chaos at the docks was beyond her.

"Hello, Jack," said Stella as she approached.

He bolted upright and adjusted his hat. "Oh, Stella. Hello. What are you doing here."

Stella held back the tears. "Jack, have you seen John? He didn't come home last night after being in town yesterday."

Jack jumped down from the wagon. "Let me think. I did see him, but I'm not sure if it was yesterday. I've been hopping what with all the new folks streaming into town."

"Please try to remember—I'm very worried."

"I can see that," said Jack as he rubbed his chin. "Yeah, I think it was yesterday—saw him coming out of the Gold Dust Exchange as I passed by."

"Did you see him after that?"

"No, I just waved as I went by and didn't see him later."

Stella began to sob quietly, taking Jack by surprise.

She was such a strong woman, having lived in Alaska long before the gold rush and been through things that would have sent most packing south. He put his hand on her shoulder.

"There, there. We'll find him. I'm sure he's fine."

"I don't want to take you away from your business."

"Don't be silly. We're going to look for him, and that's that."

Jack helped her into the wagon, then hopped up, and grabbed the reins. "Ready, set?"

CHAPTER 14

The morning sun streamed in the cafe window as Stella stared into the half-empty coffee cup. With blood-shot eyes, she looked up as Jack sat down across from her.

"We'll find him. It's just a matter of time."

"But we've looked everywhere in town. Where else?"

"Is it possible he passed the boarding house and went up the trail toward the canyon?"

"I don't see why. He was very upset about the theft, but I can't see him running off. Besides, I'm sure he would have stopped and told me."

Jack took a sip of coffee. "You need to eat. Let me get you something."

"I really couldn't. My stomach is in knots."

Jack motioned for the waiter. "I'll have the special, and bring Miss Stella here some toast and jam."

"Just in case," said Jack as the waiter retreated.

"What do we do now? We've talked to so many peo-ple, and no one knows anything."

"Well, the first thing we're going to do is get you home for some rest. Then I'll continue searching."

Stella shook her head. "I can't ask you to do that. You have a business to run."

"You can't do it on your own."

"There is one person who can help me—he found Wesley after so many years, and I know he will find John. Take me to the telegraph office."

† † †

"Well, I've had about enough," said Thomas as he plunged the shovel into the pile of gravel. "We've moved more than enough pay dirt for one day."

Sdzeè took off her gloves, slapped them together, and smiled. "You are getting lazy in your old age, Thomas Thornton."

Thomas shook his head. "You are a hard taskmaster, lady. We're making good progress—should have this winter pile of pay gravel processed before mid-summer."

"We should find a better way. It takes too much time, and we make too little gold."

"Maybe next year," said Thomas. "We should be able to afford to get some more equipment and automate things."

"That would be nice."

"Come on, let's get things stowed away here, and I'm going to make a quick trip to town to check for a letter and telegrams. You want to come along?"

"No, I will stay here and finish up my regular chores, then come up with something for your dinner."

"You sure? We could get some dinner in town."

"I am sure. You better hurry, though—be back before dark."

"You know I will," said Thomas as they walked together up the path from the creek to the cabin. "Wouldn't want to miss out on dinner—just hope I get there before closing time."

† † †

Anna was just closing the door of the post office when Thomas rode up. She turned, smiled, and brushed back her curly red hair. "Hello," she said, adjusting her skirt, her face still beaming.

Thomas reigned in the horse but didn't dismount. "Hello. I wanted to check to see if there is a letter for me. It's probably too soon, but thought I'd check anyway."

Anna motioned toward him, still smiling. "Come on in—we'll look."

Thomas tied off the horse and shuffled up the steps. Anna held the door for him but didn't step aside, forcing him to brush past her. She closed the door and made her way around to the boxes behind the counter. She sat up on the swivel stool and stared at him.

"How long have you been married, Thomas?"

Thomas shuffled his feet. "Not long."

"Are you happy with her—that...that woman from Teslin."

Thomas frowned at the implication but said nothing.

Anna leaned forward and put her elbows on the counter. "I can't believe you can be happy—living up there with her in that little shack. There are much better alternatives."

"I'm sorry, but I don't have time for this conversation," said Thomas.

"But what's the hurry? We could always—"

Thomas put up his hand. "No—what about the letter?"

Anna sat up straight. "Oh, that. A letter. Let me think."

"Don't you need to look?"

"No. There isn't anything for you."

"Why couldn't you have told me that outside?"

"Well...I thought maybe you would come in, and we could just talk for a while."

Thomas turned away from her stare—he could feel his ears turning red. "I don't have time for a chat. I need to get to the telegraph office before they close."

He stood to leave—she reached across the counter and grabbed his arm as she looked up into his eyes. "Are you sure you don't want to stay?"

He yanked his arm away and straightened his coat. "No. I don't know what ideas you have in your head, Anna, but you're wrong."

She just smiled as he backed away and opened the door. He turned and slammed the door.

Anna moved from behind the counter to the window. "You'll be back," she said as she watched him get on the horse and ride away.

Thomas breathed a sigh of relief as he nudged the horse forward. *That woman is crazy. From now on, Sdzeè goes to the post office.*

He reached the telegraph office just before closing time. It was a long shot, but maybe John had just sent a telegram rather than writing a letter. As long as he was in town, it wouldn't hurt to check.

"Afternoon," said Thomas as he entered.

Wayne looked up and pushed his glasses up on his nose. "Oh, hello, Mr. Thomas Thornton."

"Pretty formal today, eh Wayne?"

Wayne grinned. "What can I do for you?"

"Not expecting anything, but thought I'd stop by as long as I'm in town."

"No problem. I'm pretty sure we have something

here," he said, sorting through a small stack of transcribed messages. "You'd think I could remember..."

Wayne turned and grabbed a pile of messages from the desk next to the telegraph key. "Ah, here it is. From Valdez. Came in early this morning." He handed the telegram to Thomas.

Wonder what John has to say? The color drained from his face as he read.

```
THOMAS THORNTON
CHICKEN, ALASKA

JOHN IS MISSING. I DESPERATELY
NEED YOUR HELP. PLEASE COME AS
SOON AS YOU CAN.

STELLA PALMER
VALDEZ, ALASKA
```

† † †

"I will go with you," said Sdzeè, watching Thomas throw things into his pack.

Thomas shook his head without looking up. "You'll just slow me down."

Sdzeè was silent, staring at him with her hands on her hips.

The silence registered—he stopped packing and looked at her. "I'm sorry. I'd love to have your help, but I can make better time on the horse without the wagon."

"I will be worried. You tend to get into bad situations."

Thomas frowned but knew she was right—at least from her perspective. "I'll be careful."

Sdzeè lifted the gun belt holding the Colt Peacemaker from the hook next to the door. "You'll probably need this," she said.

Thomas nodded, took the gun, and put it in the pack. "I'll need the carbine too."

"What do you think happened to John?"

Thomas cinched up the pack. "I have no idea. Stella didn't give any details."

"Maybe you should wait until morning to leave."

"No, I have to leave—now. It's nearly light enough to travel all night this time of year."

Sdzeè sighed. "But dark enough to get into trouble. You will need some food to take."

Thomas shouldered the pack and grabbed the carbine from the rack above the door. "Thank you, but hurry. I'm going to have to push hard to get there."

"You should slow down. It will take nearly a week to get there."

"Not if I push it."

"You are not like the stage. They get fresh horses along the way from the roadhouse stops."

Thomas dropped the pack and slumped into the corner chair. "Stella needs me—I owe her."

Sdzeè put her hand on his shoulder. "I know. But you must be realistic. You can not kill the horse or yourself trying to get there. Besides, they may find him before you arrive."

Thomas rubbed his chin. "I hadn't thought about that."

"I will go with you. It will only add a day or two to the trip, and I can be a comfort and help to Stella while you are looking. I will feel much better being near you."

Thomas' eyes narrowed, and he started to speak, only to find Sdzeè's finger on his lips. She smiled. "I have spoken, Thomas Thornton."

He knew from experience that arguing with her once

she set her mind to something was pointless. Apart from the urgency, having her along was better than going it alone. "Okay, *shnuudeh*, you've convinced me. We leave at first light."

Sdzeè's mouth dropped open, then changed to a smile. "Where did you learn that word?"

Thomas grinned. "My secret."

"Tell me."

"A while back, I asked how to say *sweetheart* in your language. Took me a while to find someone who knew, and I've been waiting a long time to use it."

"You almost pronounced it right—enough for me to know what you said."

"I'll have to work on it."

"I like it. Now you get some sleep. I will get everything ready. We are in for long days to come."

Leaving now or in the morning won't make that much difference, he thought. He fought the sense of urgency as he watched Sdzeè scurry about, gathering more than the meager supplies he thought to pack. *I'm lucky to have her—my shnuudeh.*

† † †

Stella stared out the window of her boarding house, a cold cup of coffee in her hands. Days ago, she sent the message to Thomas—even longer since John went missing. She walked onto the porch and looked up the trail to the north, as if to will Thomas to appear. Jack spent more time than he should searching, to no avail. No one in town provided any clues. It was like he'd been swept away with the outgoing tide.

Some suggested he boarded a steamer south. Stella rejected that idea outright—it wasn't in his character to leave her, let alone without a word. Something happened to him—she was convinced. Images of her first husband's demise flooded her mind, though she could only imagine what he went through when the bear attacked. Thomas had found him—her hope now was he could do the same for John, but with a better outcome. *No, he has to be alive.*

Since John and the horse disappeared, she was stranded at the boarding house. Jack promised to bring word if anything developed, as well as check on her every few days. There were no guests at present, and the silence in the house rang in her ears. Everything would change when Thomas arrived—it was the only hope she had at the moment.

An hour passed. She exchanged the cold cup for a fresh one, returned to the porch, and sat on the bench. Though early, the spring air was already warming. The leaves popped out the week before and were nearly full. The sound of geese and sandhill cranes could be heard in the distance, winging their way north to the nesting grounds. Normally the sights and sounds of the country coming to life after a long winter would have warmed her heart. Though welcome, it wasn't enough to give her any joy.

She finished the cup of coffee and sat it on the bench. With the house empty, there was little to do each day—other than sit on the porch and wait—for John—or Thomas. Her ears strained, hoping to hear the sound of an approaching horse. Already this morning, several travelers passed by, and each time her heart leaped with anticipation, only to be disappointed.

The sun grew warm, and the long hours of worry lulled her asleep. Somewhere in the dream, he called to her. Quietly at first, then louder.

"Stella, wake up."

She stirred, then opened her eyes to see Thomas and Sdzeè standing on the stairs. She jumped up. "Thomas! You're—"

Her voice trailed off—the darkness enveloped her.

"Stella, are you okay?" said Thomas.

She opened her eyes to find Thomas standing over her, fanning with his hat. "What happened?"

"You fainted."

"I...that's never happened to me before."

Sdzeè knelt beside her and placed her hand on her arm. "When was the last time you ate?"

Stella shook her head as she started to sit up. "Not sure. Haven't felt like it."

"Today?" said Thomas.

"No, I really can't remember when."

Thomas helped her up and guided her inside to the kitchen table. "You sit. We'll get you something to eat."

Stella grabbed his hand and held tight, tears welling up in her eyes. "I'm so glad you're here."

He patted her hand. "It's going to be alright, but you need to take care of yourself."

Sdzeè was already in the kitchen, looking about.

"I can cook something," said Stella. "You're guests."

"Nonsense," said Thomas. "You sit there and don't move."

Thomas entered the kitchen. The big cast-iron stove was cold, a good sign that Stella hadn't cooked anything for a while. He opened the front and stuck his hand inside—no warmth. The coals were cold as well.

"I'll get the fire going," said Sdzeè. "Why don't you fetch some eggs." She lowered her voice and glanced at

Stella. "It might have been a while."

Thomas nodded and made his way out the back door. Fortunately, there was wood in the box next to the stove, and by the time Thomas returned with a dozen or more eggs, she had the fire going.

"I can do that," said Stella as she started to get up.

"Sit," said Thomas. "Sdzeè's happy to do it, and I don't want you hitting the floor again."

Stella sighed. "There's potatoes and onions in the root cellar if you like."

Once the stove heated up, Sdzeè turned out heaping plates of eggs with fried potatoes and onions. Fresh coffee rounded out the meal.

Stella stared at the food before her, toying with the fork. Thomas was already digging in, hungry from the last hard push on the trail.

"Stella, dear. Please—you need to eat," said Sdzeè.

"I know, but I just have no appetite."

"You'll feel better. And you need your strength if we are to find John."

CHAPTER 15

Thomas looked out across the meadow to the river as he sipped his morning coffee from the porch of the boarding house. Stella was still asleep, fatigued from the ordeal of worrying about John. A flock of geese winged their way upriver as Sdzeè stepped out onto the porch.

"What is the plan, Thomas?"

Thomas took another sip. "Not sure. We need to talk to Stella to see if we can get a clue where to start. She and Jack have already been about town looking with no results."

Sdzeè nodded, then sat down next to Thomas. She took his hand. "What if we can't find him?"

Thomas didn't want to think about what it would do to Stella—though he knew the answer. "We'll find him—one way or the other."

Sdzeè clutched her throat. "Alive?"

"We can only hope. I'm not prepared to devastate Stella with that kind of news a second time."

Sdzeè nodded.

"She mentioned a boarder that seemed overly interested in John's missing money. I need to find out more about him," said Thomas.

"Yes. His name was..."

"Tannvas—the man John mentioned in the telegram."

"Yes. That was it. And his first name was Derik if I remember correctly."

The floor upstairs creaked. "Sounds like Stella is awake," said Thomas.

"I'll reheat the coffee and pour her a cup," said Sdzeè as she turned for the door.

"How about some breakfast for your old man?" shouted Thomas.

"What old man? You are still a kid, Thomas Thornton."

Thomas laughed. "Ok, but I still need to eat---and Stella's going to need something for certain."

Sdzeè put her hands on her hips, then slowly smiled. "Fine, I will get on it."

The smile faded from his face. "This is a serious situation—we can't forget that."

† † †

As Stella came downstairs, the smell of bacon drifted up to meet her. She frowned slightly, then made her way to the kitchen.

"Come now, Sdzeè, I should be cooking for you."

"Oh, it is no problem. I am happy to do my share. I have breakfast ready for you. Call Thomas from the porch, and I will bring it to the dining room."

"But—"

"I insist. You don't always have to be the host."

Stella sighed, then smiled at her. "Ok, you win—today. I'll fetch him."

Thomas and Stella returned to the dining room and found Sdzeè already had the plates at the table, along with freshly poured cups of coffee.

"You're quick," said Stella.

"I try. That is the last of the bacon."

Stella put her hands flat on the table, tears welling up in her eyes.

"What is it?" said Thomas.

"John was on his way to buy bacon and other things when he disappeared."

Sdzeè put her hand on Stella's shoulder. "It is alright. We will find him."

Thomas placed his hand on hers. "Everything's going to be fine, but you have to take care of yourself as well."

Stella nodded and picked up her fork. "Thanks, I can't tell you how much I appreciate you coming, but I want to help, not be a burden."

"You've never been that," said Thomas. "Now eat, and between bites, tell us about the mysterious boarder."

Stella relayed the story of Tannvas, his unusual interest in the missing Palmer fortune, and the robbery of the gold and cash from the hiding place behind the wood box.

"Did you confront him about the gold?" said Thomas.

Stella nodded. "John did, and he denied having anything to do with it. John sent him packing before he finished his breakfast."

"Was he mad when he left?"

"Defiant, I would say. He didn't pay us for his stay, just slammed the door and left."

Thomas rubbed his chin. "I can't help thinking there may be some connection between him and the robbing of Van Sant's grave."

"Yes, it's quite coincidental, but we have no way of knowing for sure," said Stella. "As far as I know, he never traveled to Chicken, but it's always possible."

"We need to know what he looks like. He was about my height?" said Thomas.

"Yes, he has shoulder-length brown hair and a broad, bushy mustache."

"Anything else?"

"Nothing unique," said Stella. "He was dressed like most anyone else you'd see on the street in Valdez."

"Too bad he didn't have a big scar or walk with a limp," said Thomas. "But we couldn't be that lucky."

"So where do we start?" said Sdzeè.

"I don't know. I'm at a loss. Maybe start by talking to Jack—everything's a blur, and I can't remember everywhere we looked and who we talked to," said Stella.

"I'll ride into town and look him up," said Thomas. "Do you still have that spare saddle? I'd rather not take the wagon into town."

Stella nodded. "It's in the barn, but I think I should go with you."

Thomas shook his head. "I'll be able to get around quicker by myself, and then I'll get back to you with the plan once I talk to Jack."

Stella looked at him, then sighed. "I hate all the waiting. It grinds on your soul."

"I know. But we have to—"

"Someone's here," said Sdzeè as the sound of a squeaking wagon wheel flooded the house.

Thomas opened the door and went out on the porch, followed closely by Sdzeè and Stella. There sat Jack on his wagon, face flushed.

"Jack, I was just coming to find you. We just got here late yesterday," said Thomas. He turned to Sdzeè. "And this is my wife, Sdzeè."

"Didn't know you were here," he said as he jumped

down off the wagon. "Nice to meet you, ma'am. We need to go to town—now."

"Why? What's happened?" said Stella.

Jack took off his hat and stared at the ground, then looked up. "They found a body."

Stella staggered, grabbing Thomas's arm. "Is it...is it John?"

Jack shook his head. "Hasn't been identified yet, but I thought you should know—to be prepared just in case."

Thomas guided Stella to the chair on the porch. "Where was it found?"

"I heard it was in the woods along the trail by the river, but don't know for sure. Just got the word from a fella that passed them on the way in. They're taking it to the undertakers and should be there by the time we get to town."

"I don't want you seeing this, Stella. So, I'll go," said Thomas.

"No, I need to go."

"If it's him, there will be time to say goodbye later—if it's not, you don't need to see it."

Stella slumped further in the chair. "I guess you're right."

"Sdzeè will stay here with you. I'll ride in and get back as soon as I possibly can."

"Ok. Thank you, Thomas."

"You just take care of yourself for now. Jack, I'll saddle up and follow you."

Jack nodded and hopped up onto the seat of his wagon. "Sorry to be the one to bring news, Stella."

"I'm glad you came. We need to know."

Moments later, she watched Jack and Thomas ride away, then began to cry.

† † †

Thomas spied a large crowd in the street as he followed Jack's wagon to the undertaker's office. *Looks like the finding of a body is a spectator event.* He slid off the horse and hitched her to the rail. Jack was already off the wagon and pushing his way through the crowd.

"Move aside," he shouted as he angled his way to the door.

Thomas followed close behind him. At the door stood a tall, burly, red-headed kid—the undertaker's son—with the beginnings of what might be a beard.

"Hi, Billy," said Jack. "What's going on?"

Billy hawked a wad of tobacco on the step, barely missing Jack's boot. "Keepin' the gawkers out."

"Well, we need to get a look at the body."

Billy smiled, revealing chunks of tobacco lodged in his yellow teeth. "Daddy says no one."

"Sure, Billy, but he didn't mean us."

Billy scratched his head and looked at the door, then back at Jack and Thomas. "Ok. Go ahead," he said as he opened the door.

Jack smiled, nodded, and they entered. Billy closed the door behind them, unaware that he'd been played. Immediately the smell of death assaulted their nostrils. There was nothing like the smell of an undertaker's office—it was distinctive and heavy.

Their eyes adjusted to the dim light. No one was in the outer room, and the door to the room that served as a morgue was shut. Jack knocked—no answer. He knocked again.

"Who is it?"

"Jack."

"Jack, who?"

"Jack Yates, and I've got Thomas Thornton with me. We've come to identify the body."

The door opened, and a gnawing clenched Thomas' stomach. The undertaker motioned for them to enter. The smell was worse than the outer room, and Thomas covered his face. In the center of the room was a long narrow table, and on it, the body of a man, partially decomposed.

"You know this guy?" said the undertaker.

Thomas moved closer. The body was in poor condition, the face disfigured to the point where you couldn't tell what the man looked like. "I can't tell—can you, Jack?"

Jack leaned over and took a closer look. "Where'd they find the body? Looks like it's been out there a while."

"It was in the river, lodged against a log in the current."

"Oh? We heard it was found in the woods near the river."

"You heard wrong. A couple of boys fished him out. I figure he's been dead for nigh on a week, maybe more."

"I don't think it's him," said Jack.

"Who you looking for?" said the undertaker.

"John Palmer."

The undertaker laughed. "I know him—don't think this is him. Look at how he's dressed. This guy's practically a vagrant."

Jack and Thomas realized he was right. His clothes were well worn, and he had the remnants of a scruffy beard.

"That can't be John. Look," said Thomas, "he's much too tall."

Jack nodded. "Any identification on him?"

"Nope," said the undertaker. "Nary a slip of paper—river probably stripped everything from his pockets." He pried open the dead man's mouth to reveal stained, dark yellow teeth. "Don't think John looked like this either."

"I agree," said Jack. "It's not John."

"How did he die?" said Thomas.

The undertaker rubbed his chin, lifted the arm of the corpse, and let it drop, flailing in several directions. "See that? This guy's barely got one bone that ain't broken. Looks to me like he fell off a cliff into the river and was washed downstream."

† † †

Stella was on the porch, rocking back and forth incessantly as Thomas rode up. She saw him, jumped up, and nearly tumbled down the stairs of the porch. He could tell she'd been crying.

"It wasn't him," Thomas shouted before Stella could say a word.

She slumped to the ground and began to cry. Thomas jumped off the horse and ran to her.

"Come on, up with you," he said as he hoisted her to her feet. "It's good news."

Stella dried her eyes. "I know, I'm glad it's not him, but it could be—I mean he could be..."

"Don't think that way."

"I'm trying, but I can't seem to push the worst out of my head."

Thomas guided her up the steps and to a chair in the dining room. "Sdzeè, get Stella some water."

"Coming," she yelled from the kitchen.

Thomas heard the squeaking of the pump handle as Sdzeè filled a glass.

Sdzeè sat the glass in front of Stella. "Here you go."

Stella looked up but said nothing. Thomas had never seen her like this. She was always the strong one, even in the face of great adversity. John's disappearance had wholly unnerved her, but he could understand—having a second husband disappear was unthinkable.

Stella took a sip and set the glass down. "Who...who was it?"

"Nobody knows," said Thomas. "He had no identification on him, and so far, no one has recognized him."

"Poor fellow," said Stella.

"Yeah, nothing like dying alone in Alaska and no one knowing—or caring."

Stella groaned and started to cry again.

"Stella, I'm sorry. John is fine—I know he is. And we will find him, no matter what."

Stella wiped the tears with the back of her hand. "When?"

Thomas sat down next to her and put his hand on hers. "I'm headed back to town and try and get a line of this Tannvas fella. Someone must know where he is or if he left town."

"But we've looked all over," said Stella. "No one has seen him—or John."

"I'm going to focus on the docks. Maybe he caught a ride with a fisherman or on one of the local transports."

"Don't forget to check the steamships," said Sdzeè.

"Right. There's only been a few depart since John disappeared. Hopefully, they'll let me look at the manifests."

Stella put her head in her hands. "Check for John too."

Thomas shot a glance at Sdzeè, who shrugged her shoulders. "You don't think he left on a steamer, do you?"

"I'd like to believe that, but at this point, we have to consider all possibilities," said Stella.

Thomas didn't like the possibilities—most of them were not good. John could have been attacked by a bear and dragged away, but that didn't account for the missing horse, which surely would have escaped. He could have been waylaid by bandits on the trail, but that was rare these days. Or, he could have chosen to leave, something that Thomas thought was unthinkable. He knew the man—worked with him, and stood by him. *No, if John is missing, it's not by choice.*

CHAPTER 16

Thomas took off his hat, pulled out a handkerchief, and wiped his brow. The midday sun was hot, an unusual occurrence in Valdez early in the year. It took a fair amount of cajoling, but the agent at the Alaska Steamship Company finally allowed him to look through the manifests for the last ten days. He found nothing—no indication that John or Tannvas booked passage on a ship. He wasn't naive—anyone genuinely looking to disappear would use an alias. In retrospect, the time spent scouring the manifests was probably a waste, but at least it was clear that neither left using their real name. Nevertheless, he made stops at the other two companies to inquire, to no avail.

Thomas smoked a cigarette as he walked along the docks, pondering where to begin. No steamships were in port, and the next steamship, the *Excelsior*, wasn't due for a couple of days. That left the small lightering and transports—boats that may have given passage to either of the men. Thomas knew that destinations varied—from transporting miners to the Cliff or Ellamar mines or prospectors to the numerous small islands that dotted Prince William Sound. There was the fox farm on Goose Island and many hunting cabins scattered from Valdez all the way west to Chenega. There was no way to search them all, but Thomas was hopeful that questioning the transporters would give him a lead.

Describing John was no problem—Tannvas, on the other hand, was more difficult. All he had to go on was Stella's description—a young man with long brown hair and a broad mustache. *Not much to go on.*

"Blast it, man. I've got work to do," said the boat captain.

Thomas tipped his hat and moved on. It was the typical response to his questions—he was getting nowhere. Most were too busy or too suspicious to even give him the time of day. He looked down the long wharf that stretched out into the waters of Port Valdez. At low tide, it would be a mudflat—no boats would be moored. Now there were a dozen or more. He tired of the task but carried on for Stella's sake.

All the boats were small, with two masts at the most. Thomas shouted as he passed each, but no one responded. Finally, he reached the end of the wharf where an older craft—more like a scow—was tied off. A bearded fellow was lounging on the deck, smoking a pipe.

"Hey, mate—everyone's left for the day. I'm the only bloke still around. What can I do for ya?"

"I'm looking for a couple of fellows that may have hired a boat. Do you know John Palmer?"

The man tapped his pipe on the deck rail, sending the charred ash into the muddy water. "Can't say that I do."

"He married Stella Baird after her first husband Wesley passed."

"Aye, now I know who you mean. What about him?"

"Well, I'm looking for him. He's gone missing."

The man stroked his beard for a second. "Nah, haven't seen him recently."

"It would have been a week or more ago."

The man shook his head. "Nope."

"The other man is Tannvas—medium build with long brown hair and a broad mustache."

"Younger fella? Aye, seen that weasel, I did."

"When?"

"Musta' been four or five days ago. Wanted to buy my boat, he did."

"He wanted to buy it, not hire you?"

"Aye. I told him she's not for sale, then he shoved a jar full of gold in my face. Told him no anyway."

"That's him, I'm sure. Did he say why he wanted the boat?"

"Nope. He kept shovin' that gold at me until I threatened to run a shark hook through him."

"Did he say anything else that would give me a clue as to where he went?"

The man shook his head. "Sorry, he went away mad when I wouldn't do business."

Thomas nodded. "Thanks for the information."

Oh, you might check the saloon. He smelled like a bottle of cheap whiskey."

"I'll do that. Thanks again."

"Best of luck to you," said the man as he began restocking his pipe.

Thomas slowly walked back down the wharf toward the street. *Why would Tannvas want a boat?* He mulled it over in his mind. If he found another to purchase, he could have sailed off anywhere. The fact that he had a jar full of gold made it very likely he robbed Stella and John, but it didn't mean he knew where John was. *Maybe a dead end,* thought Thomas. He was better off focusing on John rather than chasing after Tannvas. He might recover the gold and money if he found him, but that was secondary to finding John. He decided to try the saloon before moving on.

Reaching the Bohemian Saloon that graced the street along the docks, Thomas entered, hoping to find someone who by chance sold a boat recently. The saloon was small, crowded, and noisy. The smell of cigar smoke and stale beer filled the air.

He shouted over the roar of the half-drunk fishermen, so-called captains, and women. "Anyone sell a boat recently?"

No one even looked at him. He stepped up to the bar, knowing there was one sure way to get their attention, although it would be costly. "Give me a shot of whiskey."

The bartender nodded, slapped a shot glass down on the bar, and filled it half-full. He wasn't much of a drinker, but Thomas picked it up and downed it in one gulp, then slammed it hard on the bar. No one noticed. He raised it again and began slamming it over and over in a rhythmic fashion, getting louder with each hit. Finally, the din subsided, and heads turned.

"The next round is on me if—"

The roar of the patrons filled the air. Thomas resumed the slamming of the shot glass to quiet the crowd.

"If, you will answer one question. Have any of you sold a boat to a stranger recently?"

The men looked around the room at each other—no one answered. Thomas sighed. "I'm looking for John Palmer or a young man with a broad mustache who may have paid for transport with gold."

"Nah, we ain't seem 'em, now give us our drinks," shouted a drunk from the corner table. Others chimed in and began pounding their glasses.

Thomas gave up, motioned for the bartender, and paid

him. The crowd resumed their revelry as Thomas returned to the street. As he was unhitching his horse, a
young woman in her twenties with long blonde hair and
bright lipstick exited the saloon and approached. Thomas
didn't recognize her but made a quick judgment as to her
profession.

"I think I know the man you are looking for."

"Oh? Which?"

"Well, I've met him at least once. Is his name Derik?"

"Yes, that's him."

"What do you want with him?"

"I owe him some money and want to get it back to
him," said Thomas, conjuring up a lie.

Hearing money was involved, she said, "What's it
worth to you?"

Thomas reached into his pocket and pulled out a small
leather bag. He opened the drawstring and took out a
nice, five pennyweight nugget. "This do?"

She snatched the nugget from his hand and, with two
fingers, stashed it in her convenient yet prominent hiding
place. "Told me he was staying at an old cabin up near
Goat Creek."

"You're sure he said Goat Creek?"

"Yes, blast it. What more do you want?"

Thomas looked her up and down and knew he wanted
nothing more, apart from one small thing. "Can you forget we had this conversation?"

She smiled and stuck out her hand.

Thomas removed another nugget of similar size and
dropped it in her palm. "That enough?"

Her hand snapped shut, and she whirled around. Thomas
watched as she entered the saloon. At least now he had
something to go on, and it was an area he was familiar

with. As he rode away, his thoughts turned to the day he found Wesley's remains in the valley beyond the divide of Goat Creek. He nudged the horse forward with renewed purpose. Tannvas was the only lead he had to John's disappearance, but it might be a dead end. Nevertheless, it was better than nothing. *Tomorrow I head for Goat Creek.*

† † †

"Be careful up there, Thomas," said Stella as she watched him cinch the saddle.

It was still early, but Thomas knew it would be a long day, especially if he found Tannvas. "I will. You know I've been there before."

"I know. But I still worry."

"She is right to have concern. I should go with you," said Sdzeè.

Thomas shook his head. "You need to stay here and look after Stella."

"I don't need looking after."

Thomas smiled at her. "You must admit you haven't been yourself. Sdzeè is more than happy to help around here. What if you get boarders?"

"I guess. I just hate to think of you alone up there."

Thomas secured his pack and tent to the horse and placed the .44-40 carbine in the scabbard. "I'm ready for anything."

"You are taking camping gear?" said Stella.

"Yes. It doesn't hurt to be prepared," said Thomas as he mounted up. "I'll probably be back tomorrow, but no later than the day after."

"You better be," said Sdzeè.

Stella nodded. "Thomas, please be careful."

Thomas turned the horse toward town and nudged her forward. "I will."

He looked back several times, and each time, Stella and Sdzeè waved. Finally, he rounded the bend in the trail, and the boarding house went out of sight. The trailhead to Goat Creek was about two miles from the boarding house. He remembered the route—narrow and with rocks jutting out of the ground. In places, it was largely overgrown—few people ventured that way. He wasn't sure, but it seemed like it was about five miles to the end. From there, getting to Goat Creek involved some busting through the brush before it opened up—hopefully, it wouldn't come to that.

The young lady at the saloon said Tannvas was at a cabin *near* Goat Creek. Thomas knew of the old cabin at the end of the narrow trail but wasn't aware of any others. There was nothing in the Goat Creek valley—at least not the last time he was there.

It seemed an unlikely spot for Tannvas to hide out—if that was what he was doing. When John gave him the boot, he said it wasn't over, and Tannvas' response worried him.

It was a lonely stretch of trail—there were no mining claims along the river, and Goat Creek held little or no gold. The cabin at the end was built by a miner or trapper years ago and long since abandoned. The last time he saw it, the roof was sagging badly, but the door was still in place. In a pinch, it could serve as a refuge from the elements.

It took a little over two hours for Thomas to near the end of the trail. He slowed the horse to a walk, moving slowly. He wanted to get a look at the cabin before approaching too close. Fifty yards later, the smell of smoke reached him. He pulled the horse up short, dismounted, and tied her off to a small branch next to the trail. "Stay here, girl," he said as he gently patted her neck.

Thomas stood there for several minutes, listening. Hearing nothing, he removed the carbine from the scabbard and slowly worked the lever to chamber a round. *Not going in there blind.* He patted the horse on the neck again, then moved forward, sticking to the edge of the trail for cover. He still couldn't see the cabin.

He stopped every twenty yards or so to listen, then worked his way forward. The cabin finally came into view. He crouched along the trail, a thick stand of alder sheltering him. Wisps of smoke drifted up from the chimney. *Someone's in there, but who?* He waited, unsure of how to proceed.

Fifteen minutes passed with no activity around the cabin. Hoping to get a look inside, Thomas crept closer, circling through the brush to the rear of the cabin. To his dismay, there was no window. If he wanted to get a peek inside, he would have to look in the only window—the one right next to the front door.

While it seemed likely someone was inside, there was no horse or wagon present. *Maybe they went away and left the fire going.* Deciding to risk a peek inside, he moved slowly around to the front, keeping low so as not to be seen through the window. Thomas gently placed the carbine on the ground and rose slowly, just enough to see through the lower pane. Unfortunately, the window was filthy inside and out, and the interior was dim—he couldn't see anything.

He picked up the carbine and moved around to the back of the cabin. He had to decide whether to walk in the door with the gun leveled or just knock. Either could be risky. Most folks in the bush didn't take kindly to someone busting through their door—lead was likely to

be thrown in your direction. Thomas didn't know anything about Tannvas other than what Stella told him. *No
way to know how he'll react—if he's even in there.*

He decided not to be too aggressive, moved around
to the front, and lightly knocked on the door. He waited,
then knocked a little louder. Still nothing. Taking a last
look behind him, he slowly opened the door. It took a
few seconds for his eyes to adjust to the light. He staggered back at the sight of John, bound to a chair and
gagged. His bruised face was stained with blood, his
head slumped forward.

Thomas called out quietly, but John didn't respond.
He could see his chest moving. *At least he's alive.* Thomas
leaned the carbine against the wall and stepped around
the table to reach John. A noise startled him, but as he
turned, a sharp pain shot through his head, then darkness.

CHAPTER 17

Stella placed the basket of eggs in the crook of her arm and closed the latch on the hen house. The handful of light brown eggs were more than enough for breakfast since it was only her and Sdzeè. She walked the short path back to the boarding house walked up the stairs. As she reached for the door, the sound of a horse coming up the trail reached her ears. She stopped, waiting to see who it was.

Stella screamed. The basket of eggs crashed to the ground, spilling them in the dirt. Sdzeè came running from the house.

"Stella, what is wrong?"

She pointed at the horse, trotting up the trail toward the house. Sdzeè came down the porch stairs and picked up the basket, then ran toward the horse. Grabbing the dangling reins, she led her back to Stella.

"This is bad," said Stella. "Where is Thomas?"

Sdzeè realized all the gear, except the carbine, was still lashed to the horse. That meant Thomas spent the night somewhere but without any equipment. With her hands shaking, she tied the horse to the hitching rail.

"I don't know. Maybe the horse just got away from him."

Stella shook her head. "Your horse will stay when

ground-tied. So if she was tied and broke free, Thomas must not have been near."

"Maybe something spooked her."

Stella began to cry softly. "Now they're both gone. What are we going to do?"

Sdzeè put her arm around Stella and guided her to the bench seat on the porch, then sat down beside her. She looked out beyond the horse to the trail and took a deep breath, letting it out slowly. She sympathized with Stella, both having suffered the loss of a husband in the past. Now that same gut-wrenching feeling gnawed at her.

She looked at Stella, sitting with her hands in her lap, head down, and sobbing quietly. This was the woman Thomas described as strong and resilient, yet now, she was broken. If Thomas and John were to be found, it was now up to her.

† † †

"No, you can't do this on your own," said Stella as she watched Sdzeè finish packing food and supplies. "It's too dangerous."

Sdzeè smiled. "I can handle myself. Remember?"

Stella knew what she meant. If not for Sdzeè intervening at the mining claim last year, Pierce and Cullen would have killed them all.

"I know, but this could be just as dangerous. We have to assume Tannvas is involved now, since Thomas went to the cabin where he was staying."

"I will be careful, but to be safe, I need a weapon. Thomas took the only gun we brought with us. Do you have one?"

Stella shook her head. "John had the rifle with him."

Sdzeè sighed. "Was Tannvas armed when he stayed here?"

"Yes, he had a revolver—Colt .45, I think. I don't know if he had anything else."

"Then I will have to find one somewhere. I have not been to Valdez before—is there a place to buy a rifle?"

"Yes, the general store."

Sdzeè nodded. "I need one more thing—how to get to Goat Creek."

"The trail is a couple miles from here. I will draw you a map."

"Do it quickly. I must go to town first to get a gun before I can head up there."

Stella fetched paper and pencil from the rolltop desk in the office and quickly sketched out a map, adding landmarks so Sdzeè could tell where the trail started. Sdzeè folded the map and stuffed it in her pocket.

"Thank you. I think I am ready."

"I still don't think it's a good idea for you to go alone. I don't want you to go missing too."

"I will be careful. If I can find them and Tannvas is there, I will go back to town and find help."

"You promise?"

Sdzeè nodded but knew in her heart if the time came, she would do what she had to do—if Tannvas had them, he would get what he deserved.

She finished packing and lashed the additional gear to the horse. Stella stood on the porch watching. She checked to make sure the saddle was secure, then mounted up. "I will be back in no more than two days, one way or the other."

"Please be careful."

Sdzeè nodded and turned the horse toward Valdez.

"Take care of yourself," she shouted as she nudged the horse in the ribs and galloped away.

† † †

"You're daft if you think I'm selling you a gun," said the man behind the counter at the general store.

"Why?" said Sdzeè.

"You know why. Take your business elsewhere."

"I am new here. I need the rifle."

"We don't sell guns and ammunition to your kind."

"My kind?"

The man waved his hand at her to dismiss her, then crossed his arms. She stood her ground.

"My kind—my people, have saved many of your ill-prepared from death and suffering. We have given them food and shelter, guided them, and taught them to survive in this land."

"That's not the way I see it. And never done anything for me."

"Sell the rifle to the young lady," came a voice from the corner of the store. Sdzeè turned to see Jack walking toward the counter.

The man cleared his throat. "Oh, Jack—didn't see you there. This, uh, lady a friend of yours?"

"Yes. Now give her what she wants, or I'll have words with your wife."

"Sure, no offense meant," he said. "Now, what was it you needed?"

Sdzeè looked at Jack, smiled, then turned back to the man. "I will need a .45-70 and fifty rounds."

Jack laughed. "Lady knows what she wants."

"I guess," said the man as he laid the rifle on the

counter along with two boxes of cartridges. "Big gun for a little girl."

"I am not a little girl. If you knew me, you would know what I am capable of."

The man laughed, then stiffened. "You threatening me?"

Jack stepped forward, and the man backed up from the counter. "Better be careful—I don't think she makes threats."

Sdzeè said nothing. She placed what was due on the counter, picked up the rifle and cartridges, and headed for the door. Jack gave a last look to the man, then followed behind her. Once outside, he gently grabbed her arm.

"What do you need the rifle for?"

Sdzeè relayed to him the latest—Thomas was missing after going to the Goat Creek area to look for Tannvas and John.

Jack shook his head. "This just keeps getting better and better."

"I know. And Stella is very worried, nearly frantic," said Sdzeè. "But thank you for what you did in there."

"Sure. Some people are idiots."

Sdzeè nodded. "I must get going. I want to get there before dark."

Jack tightened his grip on her arm. "I'm going with you. We'll have a better chance with the two of us."

"No, I will go—"

"Stop. I'm not taking no for an answer. If I know Thomas, he wouldn't want you going up there alone. Follow me to my office, and I'll get my gear."

"Ok. I will take your help, Jack Yates. But we must hurry."

Sdzeè mounted up as Jack jumped into the seat of the

draying wagon and whipped the reins. The horse lurched forward, and Sdzeè followed. In less than five minutes, they reached the office. He hopped down.

"You can come inside if you want—I'll only be a few minutes."

"I will wait here."

Jack entered the office and returned shortly, carrying a pack and a gun belt. "Hope I won't need this," he said, holding up the belt.

"I hope not either. Are you taking the wagon or just your horse?"

"I've been up that trail with the wagon, it's tight, but if we have to transport someone, it's our best bet."

Sdzeè hadn't thought about how she would bring Thomas or John back if they were found. "A good idea, Jack Yates."

Jack climbed up into the wagon. "Just call me Jack." He pushed up his sleeves, grabbed the reins, then looked squarely at Sdzeè, "Ready, set?"

✝ ✝ ✝

Thomas opened his eyes, trying to get them to focus. He tried to move but couldn't. Slowly his eyes adjusted to the dim light, and he realized he was inside a cabin—the cabin.

He struggled, only to find his arms and legs were bound tightly to the rickety chair. His head pounded, but he couldn't reach it to see if he was bleeding. To his right, Thomas saw John in much the same condition as before, but the blindfold was now gone.

"John. John, can you hear me?"

John moaned and slowly opened his left eye. The other was swollen shut, and he struggled to lift his head.

"Thomas? Is that you?"

"Yes. How bad are you hurt?"

"What...what are you doing here?"

"Looking for you. Are you hurt badly?"

"Apart from my head pounding, bruised ribs, and a black eye, I'm doing great."

"Is it Tannvas?"

"Yes, but that's not his name."

"Where is he now?"

"I don't know. He doesn't spend a lot of time here, except to interrogate me—and pound on me some more."

"What's he after?"

"He's convinced I either have the money or know where it is."

"What did you mean his name's not Tannvas?"

John coughed and tried to clear his throat. "He's Preston Van Sant's son."

Thomas shook his head. "What—really?"

"Yes, but I didn't recognize him. Van Sant abandoned him early on, and I haven't seen him in years."

"What makes him think you have the money?"

"Van Sant sent him a note or letter saying if anything happened to him, he would find the clue among his possessions. Since we buried him, he thinks I know something."

Thomas struggled against his bonds without success. "We have to get out of here."

"It's no use. He cinches it all tight every time he returns. He thinks he's pretty clever, right up to the name he used."

"Tannvas?"

"Yes. It's an anagram of Van Sant."

Thomas thought for a second. "It seemed like an odd name." He turned to John and lowered his voice. "Did you tell him about the slip of paper found in Van Sant's grave clothes?"

"No, it might be my only chance to recover the money."

"Stella's taking this hard. I promised to find you—Sdzeè is with her."

"I'm glad she's not alone," said John.

"We need to figure out how to get out of here."

"I'm not sure I can take another beating. I've not had anything to eat in days."

"There has to be a way to get out of here. If only—listen. Someone's coming."

The sound of a trotting horse could be heard, then rustling outside the door. Thomas and John looked at each other, then held their breath. The door slowly opened, and Derik Van Sant entered. His hair was trimmed to just above the collar. Sporting a new hat, he almost looked like a completely different man—except for the mustache still gracing his lip.

"Good afternoon gents, I trust the accommodations are treating you well."

John growled. "I see our gold and cash has done well in cleaning you up."

"Yes, it helped a lot. There's only one thing wrong—it's disappearing fast, so I'll need to know where the money is."

"You can't keep us here forever," said Thomas. "Or do you intend to kill us?"

Van Sant laughed and sat down across from them. He placed the .45 Colt on the table, pointed squarely at Thomas. "You see, that's the difference between my father and me. I'm not a murderer."

John glared at him. "I don't think we can believe anything you have to say."

"Perhaps. But I have no intention of harming either of you unless you continue to withhold what I want to know."

"Is that why that .45 is pointed at me?" said Thomas.

"A mere coincidence," said Derik as he reached down and spun it on the table.

"Let us go. We don't know anything more than you do about the money," said Thomas.

"Oh? Is that right? Tell me what you do know."

John lurched forward, nearly toppling the chair. "I'll tell you what I know. Your father was a murdering bastard, and you're cut from the same cloth."

Van Sant smiled and picked up the .45, turned it slowly toward John, then holstered it. "What about you, Thornton? I'm betting you know something, being the one that killed my father."

"You don't know the whole story. It was self-defense."

Van Sant laughed, then stood. "Frankly, I don't care. Between the two of you, you're running two gold mines and a boarding house. To me, that says you've got money, maybe in a bank, might be hidden, but somewhere."

John hissed. "You've stolen everything we had."

Van Sant looked squarely at Thomas. "Are you going to help me or not? Because I've got yet another option."

"What do you mean."

"Your adopted mother—Stella."

"I swear, if you touch her, your life won't be worth a red cent," said Thomas.

"Then I suggest you cooperate."

"And if we do, then what? You'll let us go?" said John.

Van Sant didn't answer and turned toward the door.

"Blast it! Answer me!" said John.

Van Sant stopped. "Once I'm safely away, you'll be set free."

John looked at Thomas, who shook his head slightly. Revealing the existence of the paper found in Preston's coat could mean the fortune would be lost. For John, the threat to Stella changed everything—yet Thomas seemed to be against revealing what they knew.

Van Sant looked at them and cocked his head. "Well, I'm not blind. Tell me."

John hesitated, not knowing if he could trust the man to let them go. Concern for Stella weighed heavy on him. If it would keep her safe, the money was of no consequence. Thomas looked at John and knew what was coming.

"Well? I'm growing tired of this game, so let's have it."

"We found a slip of paper, sewn into the lining of your father's coat," said John

Thomas stared at John for a second, then sighed.

"What coat? Where?" said Van Sant.

"Are you aware your father's grave was dug up and his clothes removed?" said Thomas.

"Of course. I'm the one who arranged it."

"So it was you?"

"No, a so-called associate of mine."

"Ah, well, he didn't do a very good job, did he."

"He was a dolt."

"Was?"

Van Sant's hand moved to the holster and rested on the grip of the revolver. "Never mind. Where's the paper?"

Thomas clenched his teeth. "I don't have it with me."

"Where is it? Ah, perhaps Stella has it. I may have to visit her after all."

"She doesn't have it," said John. "But I have a letter that describes it."

"Ah, the letter. You know I searched the boarding house for it while you sat like dolts at Wikidels.

"I figured you overheard Stella and me talking about it. I should have run you off the first time I found you downstairs that night."

Van Sant laughed. "Yes, you probably should have. Now, where's the letter?"

"In my saddlebag."

"Don't lie. I already went through all your stuff."

"John, don't," said Thomas.

"Quiet, Thornton," said Van Sant, resting his hand on the Colt.

"There's a false bottom—it's there."

Van Sant laughed. "Another of your fine hiding places, eh? Like that for your gold and money at the boarding house."

John tensed, then slumped back in the chair, knowing now was not the time.

Van Sant turned for the door. "I'll be back shortly. Don't go anywhere."

He let out a roar of laughter as he exited and slammed the door. They heard him ride away and waited to make sure he was gone.

"Why did you tell him about the letter?" said Thomas.

"I had to do something to get him out of here. I've got one hand free—maybe I can untie you."

Thomas scooted his chair around until he was back to back with John. "How much time do we have?"

John used his free hand to work on the knots holding Thomas fast to the chair. "He's got the horses, well mine anyway, stashed about a quarter mile up the river back in a little meadow sheltered by alders. When we first arrived, he took me there, left my horse, and dragged me back with a rope tied around both hands."

"That explains why it looked like no one was around when I got here. If it wasn't for the smoke, I'd have thought the cabin empty. We'll need horses to get away."

"He'll be back in a huff—the letter isn't where I said it was."

"Well, you better get me untied quick."

"I'm working on it, but with only one hand, it's not going well."

Thomas strained against the ropes. "Doesn't feel any looser."

"Stop moving. You're making it harder."

John worked the knot, finally getting it loose enough for Thomas to free his hand and arm. He tried to reach the knot holding his legs fast, but couldn't.

John scooted his chair over a bit to reach the other knot. "I'll have to get your other arm free first. Too bad he didn't just tie your hands together instead of lashing your arms to the side of the chair."

"Work faster," said Thomas.

"I'm trying, I'm trying."

The knot finally gave enough for Thomas to pull his arm free. He bent over and frantically worked on the knot holding his legs. Van Sant had cinched it well and Thomas couldn't get the knot to budge.

"Listen," said John. "I think I hear someone coming."

Thomas stopped. The sound was faint but moving closer. He had to get the knot untied. Looking around, he spotted a spoon on the shelf to his left. He scooted the chair as close as possible and reached up, straining to get enough height. "Blast it—can't...reach...it."

"Hurry," said John.

Stretching against the bonds with all his might, he managed to get enough of a finger on it to flip it off the shelf. It landed on the dirt floor next to him. He grabbed it, jammed the narrow end into the knot, and pried. The knot loosened, and he quickly started pulling the tag end through.

"Someone's almost here, and no doubt it's him," said John as the sound of hoofbeats grew louder.

Thomas unwrapped the rope from around his legs, tossed it aside, then jumped up and began working on the rope holding John.

"There's not enough time, Thomas. Get out of here—come back for me."

"I can't leave you, no telling what he might do."

"Hurry. I'll be fine. Van Sant needs that clue, and as long as I hold out, I don't think he'll hurt me."

The sound of the approaching horse grew louder. Thomas looked around for a weapon but found nothing. His only hope was to make it to his horse and regroup.

"I hate to leave you," he said as he reached the door. "I'll be back."

John nodded. "Go."

Thomas opened the door, looked both ways, and bolted. The door swung shut, just enough so John only caught a glimpse of him as he headed for the trees. He listened. It was quiet—no approaching horse, no footsteps.

The noise startled him, and he nearly fell over backward in the chair. Two shots, in rapid succession from just outside the cabin, then nothing.

CHAPTER 18

John blocked the backhand with his free arm, but it didn't stop the attack. Derik pivoted behind the chair and put him in a chokehold. John slumped, Derik released the hold, then secured John firmly to the chair, pulling the knot tight enough to nearly cut off circulation. He backed away and sat in the chair across from him, waiting.

John moaned, then opened his eyes, the room slowly coming into focus. He tried to lift his free arm, only to find it was securely tied to the side of the chair.

"Where...where's Thomas?"

Derik put his feet up on the table and took a long drag on the cigarette hanging from his lips. "Thomas who?" he said, then laughed.

"Did you kill him?"

"Humph. Now, where's the letter? And this time, don't lie to me."

"I lied. There is no letter."

Derik pulled the Colt from the holster and set it on the table, the muzzle pointed squarely at John's chest. "Now you are lying, Palmer. Thornton's reaction when you mentioned it made it clear it exists."

John sighed. "I'll tell you what it said."

"Not good enough. You've already lied to me—I want to see it."

"When you tell me what's happened to Thomas, I'll tell you."

Derik snuffed out the cigarette on the table. "You're really in no position to bargain. If you don't cooperate, my next stop is to see dear, sweet Stella."

John strained against the ropes. "You stay away from her, or so help me, I'll put you in the ground."

Derik laughed, then sat up straight. "I like you, John. You've got a great sense of humor."

John sighed and sunk back into the chair. In his heart, he knew that Stella was worth far more to him than any money. "If I cooperate, will you give me your word you'll leave us alone?"

"I have no interest in harming you or Stella, so yes. Thornton, on the other hand, is another matter. He killed my father, and for that, he will pay."

John sat up straight. "So he is alive."

Derik realized his ruse was up. "Probably. I fired at him as he was crashing through the thick brush—don't know if I hit him or not, but I was more interested in making sure you hadn't gotten loose."

John felt a glimmer of hope—Thomas would come for him—and bring reinforcements.

"Why do you care about revenge? Your father abandoned you and your mother—wanted nothing to do with you for years."

"It's a matter of family honor."

John laughed out loud. "Honor? That is truly a joke."

"Careful, Palmer. Don't get on my bad side."

"Seems I'm already there."

"Enough. Where's the letter?"

"It's in the saddlebag."

"Don't lie to me again. I mean, I appreciate a clever

ruse, but you're not in a position to toy with me."

"I'm telling the truth this time. There's a slit along the inside of the bag, just below the flap under the seam."

Derik picked up the Colt and holstered it. "You better not be lying this time, or I would hate to think of what awaits Stella."

"I swear—I'm telling the truth."

Derik moved around the table and behind John's chair, causing John to flinch. Then, Derik began working on the ropes that held his legs.

"What are you doing?" said John.

"Since Thornton got away, did you think I'd just sit here and wait for him to come back with guns and a bunch of friends?"

"Where are we going?"

"First, we're going to where the horses are tethered, and if the letter isn't there, you're going on a long dark journey from which you won't return."

"Is that a fancy way of saying you're going to kill me?"

"You're smarter than you look," said Derik as he blindfolded John, tied his hands in front, and propped him up.

"Where are you taking me?" said John as Derik shoved him for the door, nearly causing him to fall face first.

"Someplace where no one will think to look for you."

† † †

By the time Jack and Sdzeè reached the turnoff to Goat Creek, the shadows were growing long. Sdzeè was impatient, knowing she could travel much faster on horseback than Jack could with the wagon. Neither of them had any idea what Tannvas looked like—she could pass him on the trail and be none the wiser. Charging ahead alone was dangerous—she resigned herself to the slower pace. At the rate they were going, it would likely be dark by the time they reached the area of the cabin.

They turned off the trail from town onto the narrow path to Goat Creek. Sdzeè remembered Thomas had told her the trail was rarely used except by hunters, and even then, it saw few travelers. As she followed the wagon, the pace slowed even more.

"Can you go any faster?" she shouted ahead to Jack.

"Not really. This trail is barely wide enough for the wagon," said Jack as he ducked under one of many over-hanging alder branches.

"It will be dark by the time we get there. How far is it?"

"About four miles to the cabin, I think."

"I hope you brought a lantern."

Derik tied a lead from the halter of the other horse to his saddle horn, then mounted up and started the trek to the new hiding place.

John struggled to free his hands, but they were firmly tied together and bound to the saddle horn of his horse. He couldn't see but knew Van Sant was in front leading his horse along a path—to somewhere.

"Stop struggling," said Derik as he looked back. "What are you going to do if you get loose—run through the woods blindfolded and bound?"

John grunted, then drooped his shoulders. "Where are we going?"

Derik laughed. "You'll see when I take your blind-fold off. You might as well relax. It's going to be a while."

By waiting until early evening, Van Sant hoped to avoid meeting anyone on the trail. They would move slowly, stopping every hundred yards or so to listen. Once they crossed the main trail, the plan was to ford the Lowe River under cover of darkness and proceed east along the south bank.

"Where are we going?" said John, louder this time.

Derik pulled the reins tight, stopping the horse, then pulled on the lead to bring John's horse alongside. John felt cold steel against his temple.

"I suggest you shut your mouth. If you don't keep quiet, I'll make sure you see the end of your wife before you get yours."

John nodded, the threat against Stella vivid in his mind. Derik returned the Colt to the holster, then nudged the horse forward.

"Did you find the letter?"

"Yes, and as bad as I want you to read it so you can tell me what that gibberish means, it'll have to wait—for now."

They made their way slowly along the trail—slower than Derik liked but out of necessity. He guessed it was at least eight miles to the hiding place, which meant it would take most of the night to get there as slow as they were going.

Derik ducked as he went under the overhanging spruce branch, then let out a chuckle as it hit John squarely in the forehead, nearly knocking him to the ground.

"Blast it!" shouted John as blood trickled down his forehead.

"Shut up!" said Derik.

"Take off the blindfold so I can see what's coming at me."

Derik shook his head, then realized John couldn't see him. "No."

"Then I'll scream every time I get whacked."

Derik sighed, then reached out and ripped the blind-fold from him, smearing blood across his face.

"I'm bleeding."

"You'll live. Now keep quiet," said Derik, knowing the blindfold would have to go back on at some point.

Darkness descended, but the moon was enough to light the way. The pace was even slower now, and though tired and hungry, Derik remained vigilant. John sat in the saddle with his head down, weaving from side to side as the lack of sleep threatened to win out.

The light flickered through the trees in the distance, and Derik thought he heard voices. He poked John, then held one finger up to his lips. John jerked his head up to look, then saw the light. He opened his mouth to speak, but Derik quickly drew the Colt and pointed it at him. John hung his head.

Derik quickly looked for a hiding place—the closest possibility was a thick stand of alders that lined the trail ahead—twenty feet behind the trees was a small clearing. He carefully turned his horse off the trail and wound their way behind the alders to the dark clearing. The brush was thick enough to hide them but not so thick that he could manage a partial view of the trail.

Derik kept the Colt at ready and stared through the trees as the voices grew louder. There was only one rea-son anyone would travel this trail in the dark—they were looking for Palmer and Thornton.

John stared through the trees, trying to see who it was and hoping it wasn't Stella. She was a tough woman, and he wouldn't put it past her to try and effect a rescue, though the thought sent a chill through him.

The light flickered brightly through the alders, and Derik leaned to the side for a view. It was one man in a wagon, followed by someone on a horse. A lantern swung from a hook mounted beside the seat. The swinging glow made it difficult for Derik to recognize either of the travelers.

Despite the gloom, John knew exactly who was driving the wagon. He caught a glimpse of the face as the lantern swung in a fortuitous direction. He leaned forward as if it would make it easier to see through the darkness, yet he couldn't clearly see the rider that followed.

They were directly across from them now, only twenty-some feet of thick brush separating them. Derik shoved the muzzle of the Colt into John's ribs, and he nearly cried out. The pair were silent as they passed, and in the last instant, John realized who the other rider was—Sdzeè.

The urge to call out was overwhelming, but he knew the outcome would be deadly—for him and perhaps Sdzeè. John was thankful Van Sant chose to remain quiet instead of ambushing them, and for that, his silence was worth it. He watched as the flickering light grew smaller, then faded from view. Five minutes later, their journey resumed. Van Sant picked up the pace to put some distance between them.

"Who was that?" said Derik after they rode for several minutes.

"I don't know," said John. "Didn't recognize either of them."

"Really? I'm pretty sure one of them was a woman. Maybe you got a woman out searching for you."

"I think you shot the only person that was looking for me."

"Thornton? Maybe. He's either dead out in the brush, bear food, or he'll be back. We may never know."

John sneered. "You're such a caring human being."

"I have my moments," said Derik. "Now shut up and ride."

CHAPTER 19

"Looks dark," said Sdzeè as she crouched beside the wagon, a good hundred yards from the cabin.

Jack nodded. "They might be in there, or we might be on the wrong track."

"What do we do now?"

"Let's move your horse and the wagon back down the trail a bit, then sneak up there and see if we can hear anything."

Sdzeè led the horse while Jack drove the wagon back down the trail until they found a spot to tie them off. Sdzeè pulled the .45-70 from the scabbard, checked to ensure it was loaded, then grabbed a handful of cartridges from the saddlebag.

"I am ready."

"Let's move slowly and quietly. If we're lucky, they'll be asleep."

They moved forward, stopping every few feet to listen. The moon illuminated the path to the cabin, casting a dim glow across the ground. Jack ducked down as he closed the gap—Sdzeè followed close behind with the .45-70 at ready. He stopped ten feet from the cabin and motioned for Sdzeè to move toward the window. She understood and crawled up to the window on her hands and knees. She stopped for a moment, then raised up, her eyes barely above the sill of the window.

The moonlight reflected off the dirty glass of the window, making it impossible to make out anything inside. The only thing she could be certain of—there was no light inside. She crouched and made her way back to Jack.

"Can not see anything. It is completely dark," she whispered.

Jack nodded. "I guess we'll need to bust in and see who's home."

"Maybe we wait until it is light? It will be hard to see anything when we enter."

"We could, but that's a long wait. I'd rather get it over with."

"I will follow you," said Sdzeè.

Jack moved slowly to the door and stood to the left. Sdzeè took up a position on the right. Jack paused, wondering if they should burst in or take a stealthy approach. He wrapped his fingers around the door handle and pulled ever so slightly. The hinges made a slight creaking sound, but the door didn't budge.

Jack motioned for Sdzeè, she moved closer, and he whispered in her ear, "We're going to have to break it down."

Sdzeè nodded and stepped aside. Jack took a couple of steps back then lunged forward, smashing his shoulder against the door. It gave way, and he crashed through, lost his balance, and fell, losing his sidearm in the process. Sdzeè was instantly behind him, the .45-70 leveled in the darkness.

"Don't shoot! Don't shoot!" came the voice from the corner of the cabin.

Sdzeè froze. "Thomas?"

"Sdzeè? Is that you?"

Sdzeè rushed forward, nearly tripped over the table in the dark, and found her way to Thomas. He was slumped in the corner, his back to the wall. Sdzeè knelt beside him. "What are you doing here? Where's John?"

A groan came from behind her. In the commotion, she forgot all about Jack. "Jack, are you alright?"

"I'll be fine once I get myself off the ground. Tend to Thomas."

"Thomas, are you hurt?"

"I...I've been shot."

"Shot? Where?" In the dark, she struggled to find the wound. "Jack, get the lantern from the wagon—quickly, please."

"The bastard got me in the arm. It's not too...uh...bad. I think I got the bleeding stopped."

"Which arm," said Sdzeè as she searched for the wound.

"Left. Just below the shoulder."

Jack returned with the lantern and hung it from a nail in the wall. In the yellow, flickering light, he could see Thomas' blood-soaked shirt. Sdzeè grabbed the sleeve and ripped it open, then gasped. The .45 caliber slug had torn a large hole through his triceps, but she couldn't tell if it struck bone.

She gently lifted his hand while supporting his elbow. Thomas let out a groan.

"Is it broken?" said Jack.

Sdzeè gently lowered his arm. "I don't think so."

"No, it's not broken, just got a nice flesh wound," said Thomas.

"You're still bleeding a little."

"I used some rope that was laying around to make a tourniquet, but I took it off a bit ago."

"We need to bandage it with something," said Sdzeè.

"Here, use this," said Jack as he pulled out his hand-kerchief. "It's clean. I washed it last year."

Thomas laughed, then winced in pain. "Don't make me laugh."

Sdzeè wrapped his arm, careful not to make it too tight. "How does that feel?"

Thomas flexed his arm slightly, groaned, then nod-ded. "It'll do."

"Now, tell us what happened and where's John."

"Help me to the chair," said Thomas. "Don't think I can get up off the floor with just one wing."

Jack and Sdzeè helped him up and got him into the chair—the same chair he was bound to hours earlier.

"John was here, but he's gone. Van Sant blindfolded him and rode off."

"Van Sant?" said Sdzeè.

Thomas explained the use of the anagram and Derik's true identity.

"Not another Van Sant," said Sdzeè. "How did you get shot?"

"Wait, you should have passed them on the trail," said Thomas.

Sdzeè looked at Jack. "We saw no one. How long ago did they leave?"

"I'm not sure. I've been fading in and out."

"Never mind that now—tell us what happened."

Thomas nodded and began the story of how he found John, was captured and tied up, and escaped, only to be shot as he scrambled through the brush to get away from Van Sant. Fearing he would be followed, he continued moving away from the cabin several hundred yards be-fore stopping to listen. Slowly he worked his way around and approached the cabin from the opposite direction. There he hid, waiting and listening, but unable to intervene.

"It was killing me that I couldn't get back in there and help John, but I only had one arm, was bleeding, and had no weapons."

Sdzeè took his hand. "Weren't you afraid he would find you?"

"That didn't enter my mind. I didn't have a plan but hoped I could come up with something. That's when I saw them leave."

"Was John okay?"

"Apart from the bruises from being beaten, he seemed like it."

Jack sat down in the other chair and removed his hat, then leaned forward. "So what's this really all about, Thomas?"

"Van Sant wants the money that his father stole from John. He thinks we know where it's at. Look, we need to get out of here and find John."

"It's no good in the dark," said Jack. "Based on what I know about this guy so far, he could be lying in ambush for us."

"Jack is right. We know that for now, John is alive," said Sdzeè.

"He'll probably keep him that way until he gets what he wants, then there's no telling what will happen—but I can guess," said Thomas.

"Did you tell him about the clue?" said Sdzeè.

Jack looked at her. "Clue?"

"We found a paper in Van Sant's grave clothes after someone dug him up. It had a cryptic note that could be a clue to find the money," said Thomas.

"Where's the paper now?" said Jack.

"We left it at the boarding house—I have it memorized."

"So that's why he's holding John—he wants the clue?" said Jack. "Why not just tell him what it is?"

"He won't believe it unless he sees it in writing—which he probably has now that John gave him the letter in which I described it."

"Then we must hurry and find him," said Sdzeè.

"Unless Van Sant knows what the clue means, I think John will be safe—but you're right—we need to find him, and quick."

"Do you have any idea where he was going? Did he say anything that might give us an idea?" said Jack.

"Maybe, but I'm tired and hurting—my head feels like it's in a fog."

"We'll rest here and head out before first light," said Jack.

Thomas started to stand, stumbled, and nearly fell before Sdzeè caught him. "We need to go find John—now."

Sdzeè helped him back into the chair, then shook her finger at him. "You are in no condition to go anywhere tonight, Thomas Thornton. And it is not safe."

Thomas sighed, knowing she was right.

"We should be able to pick up their trail at first light," said Jack. "Two horses moving close together should be fairly easy to follow."

"I hope so," said Thomas. "I really hope so."

† † †

Derik stopped as he neared the intersection with the Valdez-Eagle trail. This was the riskiest part of the journey—to be seen by anyone would be problematic. He pulled out his pocket watch but couldn't read it in the moonlight. Fumbling around in his vest pocket, he found a match, struck it, and looked at the time—nearly 11 p.m.

Still concerned that they were possibly being followed, he didn't wait long. He turned his horse to get closer to John.

"What now?" said John as he watched Derik reach into his pocket.

"I've got to blindfold you again."

John pulled back, and Derik grabbed him by the collar then yanked him forward. "Best settle down. Remember, I can always get what I want from Stella—maybe a little more."

"Leave her alone. I'll cooperate."

Derik cinched the blindfold tight, listened one last time, and hearing nothing, turned right on the trail, headed for Valdez.

"Going to town, are we?" said John.

Derik dismounted and tied his horse off to the nearest tree. "Shut up."

He grabbed a low-hanging spruce branch and bent it down. It broke with a loud crack but didn't come free. Derik cursed at the sound then proceeded to twist it until it came free. Walking back up the Goat Creek trail a few feet, he covered their tracks back to the main trail. He swept the branch back and forth, eliminating the pair of tracks. To make sure, he swept the ground in both directions along the main trail as well. There were plenty of tracks from travelers—it wouldn't take much to disguise theirs among them.

Satisfied, he tossed the branch aside, untied the horse, and mounted up. Derik kicked the horse in the ribs, and the pair broke into a gallop. Once they reached the next turnoff, the journey would be slow going, and he planned to spend as little time as possible on the main trail.

John thought they were headed for Valdez, but he could see very little out the bottom of the blindfold. He could see the saddle, a bit of ground rushing by, and his hands firmly bound to the saddle horn. He tried to twist his head and shrug his shoulders to move the blindfold, but it was no use. There was nothing he could do—no way to leave breadcrumbs for his rescuers to follow. He tried to estimate how far they had traveled by counting the sound of the hoofbeats but lost count and gave it up.

After a little over a mile, Derik slowed the horses and turned left off the trail. Here there was no trail, and they made their way through the stand of spruce and poplar to the bank of the Lowe River. They had to ford the river, and Derik led the horses upstream, looking for a suitable spot. The darkness made it difficult to find a decent crossing. Being a braided river, there were several channels of water to cross to make it to the other side. One thing was in his favor—the melt of snowpack and glaciers in the high country hadn't started yet. The river was low but still swift in places.

Another hundred yards upstream led him to a spot that looked feasible. The bank had disappeared, and it was a gentle slope to enter the river. Crossing with two horses tied together could be tricky, but Derik had no choice. He stopped at the edge.

"Alright, Palmer. Hold on tight—we're going to get a little wet. Whatever you do, don't fall off the horse."

John could hear the rushing water—he knew how tricky the Lowe River could be. "Don't do this—this is insane crossing in the dark."

"Keep your voice down, or I'll gag you as well."

They entered the river, and the water came up quickly

to just below the knee on the horses. In the moonlight, the gravel bar mid-river appeared, roughly twenty yards away. The horse hesitated, and Derik kicked her in the ribs. They continued, and the water rose to the horse's belly. The cold, muddy, swift water swirled around them as the horses snorted and tried to turn. Derik kicked harder, and his horse lunged forward, reaching the gravel bar and dry ground.

In the dark, it was difficult to tell how much further to the other side. It was nothing but open water between the gravel bar and the far bank.

"This is crazy," said John. "You're going to get us killed."

Derik laughed but said nothing. He wasn't about to let Palmer know how scared he was to continue. It was either go forward or turn back—with no plan and the prospect of being caught. *Forward we go.*

They moved forward into the water, shallower this time, and as they proceeded, it became clear there were several narrower channels ahead. As they crossed the last of them, the water was only ankle deep—the deepest channel turned out to be the first one. Reaching the other side, a new challenge met them—the bank was nearly four feet high and lined with dense alder—far too high for the horses to negotiate as they stood in the water.

Derik cursed himself for not scouting the route in the daylight but knew that, at the time, it wasn't an option. He looked up and down the river, hoping to find an exit. The horses were anxious, nervously stepping back and forth. In the dark, he had to make a choice—he chose to continue upstream to find a way out of the river.

They traveled slowly for what seemed like forever until the bank transitioned into a little beach of river rock, and the trees thinned. The horses needed no invitation, leaving the river without Derik pointing them in the right direction. They continued back from the edge for a short way to a small meadow lined with spruce and birch. Derik dismounted and tied off both horses, untied the rope binding John to the saddle horn, and yanked him to the ground. He let out a groan as the air escaped his lungs, and he struggled to catch his breath.

"You're fine," said Derik as he wrapped the dangling rope around John's wrists and knotted it tight. "We'll rest here a bit before continuing."

"Can you take off the blindfold," John asked after finally gaining his breath.

Derik thought for a moment as he looked across the river. Though Valdez was at least two miles away to the west, he could see the outline of the docks. "Nah, I think not—not yet."

John sighed. "How much longer?"

"You'll know when we get there."

John could smell the cigarette, and it nearly made him nauseous. He hadn't eaten in a day and couldn't remember his last drink. "I need water—and food."

Derik grunted, reached into the saddlebag of John's horse, and pulled out a canteen. He opened it and tipped it up over John's face, letting the water slowly pour out. The water went up his nose, he coughed, then maneuvered his mouth under the stream. After several swallows, he pulled away, the water running down the front of his shirt. Derik laughed and closed the canteen.

"No food until we get to where we're going. Let's go."

After getting John situated on the horse, they headed east along the river, zigzagging through the stands of alder, spruce, and birch. With no trail to follow, it was slow going. However, it wasn't long before they came across an old trail, largely overgrown with alder but still passable. Through the trees, roughly a half-mile away, he could see the Lowe River.

Derik dismounted and walked a short distance down the trail, looking for tracks. He found a few, but they were moose—a cow and a calf and a set of huge grizzly tracks, imprinted in the dirt. He instinctively put his hand on the Colt .45, but then noticed the bear tracks were old, dotted with little sprigs of grass. *Nothing to worry about there.*

Derik realized he could have stayed on the trail from town until he came to the mining trail, but that would have meant being exposed for much longer—if he could even have found the overgrown turnoff. *No, this way is safer.*

He estimated it was another three miles before the final turn. At the rate they were going, it would be light by then. He was anxious—anxious to read the letter's contents, but it would have to wait.

In the dark, a smile spread across his face. *Another day or two, and this is over.*

Thomas groaned as Sdzeè and Jack helped him up on the wagon. It was light enough to head out—hopefully picking up Van Sant's trail on the way. It was a chilly morning, and to make things worse, the group had to start the day without either breakfast or coffee.

"You take the lead, Sdzeè," said Jack. "You'll be able to see better than I can from the wagon seat."

Sdzeè nodded and mounted up. "We are going to need supplies if this chase goes on long."

Thomas swayed in the seat. "I...I could use some coffee—and a piece of Stella's blueberry pie."

"You need proper bandaging and rest more than anything," said Sdzeè as she nudged the horse forward.

"Right," said Jack. "Maybe we should take him to the boarding house and regroup."

"No, No," said Thomas. "You'll lose the trail."

"Alright, let's see where this leads us and then decide our next step," said Jack.

Sdzeè nudged the horse forward. "I agree. We will go a little farther and see."

At first, it was easy to track the pair of horses. From the spacing, Sdzeè could tell they were moving slowly. In the early morning light, the overhanging trees often shadowed the trail. Several times Sdzeè stopped and dismounted to get a closer look. It was slow going, and the sense of urgency made her want to move faster than was prudent.

It wasn't long before the tracks left the trail and returned. Confused, Sdzeè motioned for Jack to stop the wagon. She dismounted and bent down to get a closer look, then stood and walked off the trail and disappeared.

"What's going on?" said Jack as he lost sight of her.

Sdzeè didn't answer, but a moment later came jogging back to the trail. She stopped next to the wagon and leaned against it as she caught her breath. A shiver overtook her as she realized the significance.

"What's the deal?" said Jack. "You alright?"

Sdzeè nodded. "Yes, but we might not have been."

From the wagon, Thomas put his hand on her shoulder. "What do you mean?"

"Van Sant and John left the trail here and stopped beyond in a meadow, then returned to the trail."

"Wonder why."

"I am pretty sure they were hiding there as we passed on the trail. There is no other reason to leave the trail here."

Jack nodded. "You're right. He could have ambushed us."

"Devil it!" said Thomas. "John was right there, and you missed him."

"So close, but we had no way of knowing," said Jack.

Sdzeè grabbed the saddle horn and swung up onto the horse. "We will find them, But we must be careful. Next time Van Sant may not restrain himself."

They had little difficulty following the tracks until they reached the intersection with the main trail. Then it became clear what Van Sant did—sweeping the trail to hide their tracks. Sdzeè hopped down, trying to determine which way they went. Already there were tracks in the swept area from early morning travelers.

"It is swept in both directions," she said as she walked beyond the swept area in both directions, looking for the telltale sign of the two horses. "I can not tell."

Thomas and Jack got down from the wagon and looked over the scene.

"It would have been easier if we had gotten here before everyone walked all over it," said Thomas, cradling his left arm.

A cold rain started to fall, lightly at first, then steady. They watched as the rain hit the ground, slowly erasing all evidence of travel.

"Blast it!" said Thomas. "When will we get a break?"

Sdzeè mounted up and trotted down the trail toward town, bent over and staring at the ground, hoping to get a hint as to which way Van Sant went. After fifty yards, she stopped, turned around, and did the same in the other direction.

"I find nothing," she said as the rain pelted her.

"I failed," said Thomas. "I should have been more careful."

"This is getting us nowhere," said Jack. "Let's get to Stella's before we're completely soaked to the bone."

Thomas struggled up into the wagon on his own, and Jack took the reins. They turned toward the boarding house. "We'll regroup and figure out something," said Jack.

Thomas pulled his hat low, the rain dripping off the brim. He turned and looked behind the wagon, then back. "I hope so, but how can I face tell Stella?"

† † †

Derik pushed harder through the thick brush lining the old mining trail as it wound toward treeline. The rain stopped nearly an hour ago, but the leaves on the brush were like thousands of little sponges that shed their water when disturbed. John was wet and shivering, his teeth chattering. His wrists were sore and bloody from being bound to the saddle horn, and the cold had caused his muscles to seize.

Derik wasn't sure how much further it was but knew they were getting close. As they reached treeline, he stopped and looked back down the narrow valley. The mountain tops were hidden by clouds on both sides, and below he could see the Lowe River. Beyond it, barely a speck in the distance, was a white frame house that he recognized instantly—the boarding house. He smiled, a great sense of satisfaction in knowing that his new hiding place was in sight of Palmer's house. He could stand in full view, wave his arms, and never be seen from the speck of a house below.

"I'm freezing," said John, visibly shaking now.

"You should have dressed warmer," said Derik. "Don't worry, we're almost there."

"Where?"

"Your new home. I can see it now."

John bent his head back as far as he could, hoping to get a peek under the blindfold. Unfortunately, it was too tight, and he couldn't see anything other than a glimpse of the green around him. He could tell they were moving uphill.

They crossed the small stream that ran down the valley and turned left, arriving at a small level spot. In the middle stood a dilapidated log cabin. A bent sheet metal flue without a cap protruded from the grass-covered roof. Derik rode around the cabin, surveying the new hiding spot. He knew there was a cabin in the valley, but now that he'd seen it, the condition was a bit of a shock.

On the steep slope, thirty yards above and just below the clouds, was an adit—an entrance to the abandoned prospect. The waste rock formed a flat spot—outside the portal to the mine. A twisted set of rusted, narrow rails protruded from the opening.

Derik rode around to the front of the cabin, tied off both horses, untied John's hands, then yanked him down. He grunted, but the soft alpine tundra broke his fall.

"We're here," said Derik as he pulled John up by the collar, pushed the door open, and shoved him in.

Without a single window, the cabin was dark. Derik's eyes adjusted to the light, and he surveyed the furnishings—which were primitive. Along the back wall were two bunks, one above the other. Everything was crafted from crude spruce logs cut from the valley below. Table and chairs were absent—a bench ran the length of the right wall and along the left was a waist-high shelf next to a rusty barrel stove.

The musty, earthen smell of the long-closed cabin was nearly overwhelming. Derik guided John to the lower bunk and tied him to the support, then removed the blindfold. John's eyes adjusted, and through the open door, he got a partial glimpse of a river far below, but it provided no clue as to where he was.

"Where are we?"

"Someplace safe from your friends," said Derik. "Don't go anywhere."

"Funny," said John as he surveyed his raw and bruised wrists.

Derik left and returned shortly with a lantern and blankets. He set the lantern on the shelf, lit it, then placed one of the blankets around John's shoulders.

"See, I'm not a monster."

John said nothing as he hunched over, trying to get warm.

Van Sant leaned against the wall and pulled the letter from his vest pocket. "Now, let's see what this says."

✝ ✝ ✝

CHAPTER 20

Stella leaped from the bench on the porch and ran down the stairs as she saw the wagon approaching. She barely acknowledged Jack and Thomas on the seat as she ran past and looked in the empty wagon.

"John?" she said, her voice wavering.

Thomas slipped down from the seat and put his good arm around her as she started to cry. "Jack and Sdzeè almost had him, but don't worry, he's still alive."

Thomas guided her back to the porch while Sdzeè and Jack tied off the horses. They joined them, and the three related everything that happened—Thomas told of finding John, escaping, and how Jack and Sdzeè passed John in the night. Stella sat silent, listening, her tears drying. When they were done, she looked out at the mountains across the river. They waited.

"Thomas, let's get you inside and tend to that wound," she said as she stood.

They looked at each other, wondering at the change in demeanor.

"We're going to find him—alive," said Thomas.

Stella took him by the hand and guided him into the front room. "Wait here," she said and disappeared into the storeroom beyond the kitchen.

Thomas gave a quizzical look at Jack. Sdzeè shrugged.

"I think she might be in shock," said Jack.

Stella returned, clean cloth and antiseptic in hand. "I'm not in shock—we have work to do."

Thomas smiled. Her resolve had returned. "That's the Stella I know and love."

Stella blushed, then set about removing the bandage from his arm. "This isn't the first time I've had to tend to a gunshot wound with you."

"I know."

"So stop getting shot, and let's talk about how we're going to find John."

"We know he turned onto the trail after leaving the Goat Creek trail, but we don't know which way," said Sdzeè.

Stella thought for a moment. "They didn't come this way."

"How do you know?" said Thomas.

"Because I couldn't sleep, so I sat outside on that bench all night, watching—waiting. No one passed from either direction until daylight this morning."

"Well, that's something," said Jack. "So they must have turned toward Valdez—there's nowhere to hide between here and the Goat Creek turnoff."

"Why would he go to town?" said Sdzeè.

"Doesn't make sense," said Thomas. "He'd attract a lot of attention, especially if he's dragging John along."

"So where could he have gone?" said Stella.

"I guess we're going to have to ride the trail and try to figure it out," said Jack.

"We should go to town and ask around in case he stashed John somewhere and showed up," said Thomas.

"I'm not sure you're fit to go anywhere," said Stella.

Thomas smiled at her. "Okay, mother, fix me up with a sling, and I'll be good to go."

"Let's split up when we get to town so we can cover more ground, then rendezvous at my office later," said Jack.

Thomas and Sdzeè nodded.

"I'm going with you," said Stella.

"I think you should stay here—in case John comes back and needs help," said Thomas.

Stella nodded. "At this point, I'm not sure that will happen, but you're right."

"We'll get word to you as soon as we know something," said Jack. "Even if I have to send a messenger out to you."

Stella went to the kitchen and pulled the cast-iron skillet from the shelf. "You all need to eat something, sit down, and I'll have it ready before you can say 'Jack Robinson'."

"Good," said Thomas. "I'm starving."

† † †

"What does it mean?" shouted Derik as he waved the letter in front of John's face.

"I don't know. Your father wrote it."

"Your Destiny lies on the NP before you leave? What kind of nonsense is that?"

"I honestly can't help decipher it. You know everything I do now."

"Blast it!" said Derik as he slammed the letter down on the shelf.

"Your father always thought he was pretty clever—always had a plan—a scheme."

"Do you think it's a clue to the money?"

John shrugged. "Obviously you thought he left a clue, or you wouldn't be here."

"Don't get smart," said Derik as he sat down on the bench and lit up a cigarette.

Derik leaned back against the rough log wall. From his vest pocket, he took out the wrinkled paper that motivated him to begin the search. He reread it—no clues, just a mention of the money and, if he was clever, he could find it. That was it—the obscure clue from the grave clothes was all he had to go on. Someone must know what it meant—how to unravel it.

He returned the paper to his pocket and picked up the letter. "You're sure you don't know what it means? If you're hiding something or lying to me, it won't go well—for you or Stella."

"Honestly, I can't help you. Can you let me go now?"

"And what will happen if I do? You'll have me thrown in irons at the first chance."

"No—all I want is for you to leave us in peace. I'll make sure you have the chance to leave Valdez."

Derik shook his head and eyed John. "You seem in a hurry to get me to leave. You know something—the clue must mean the money is here—in Alaska."

"No, no. We don't know anything. That clue means nothing to us."

"I think you are lying."

"What can I do to convince you?" said John.

"Nothing—for now."

John sighed and hung his head. The days of captivity had worn him down. He was weak—even if he managed to get loose, there was no way he could overpower Van Sant, let alone make his way home.

Derik put on his hat and headed for the door.

"Where are you going?"

"Never mind. Don't get any ideas—I'll be back in a few minutes."

He slammed the door, and John listened as his footsteps retreated. The sound grew faint, and John waited to hear the sound of a horse leaving, but it didn't come. Wherever he was going, he was on foot.

John thought about the clue, wracking his brain for any hint that might solve the puzzle. The curious thing about it was the word destiny—capitalized—as was NP—an abbreviation? Surely this was significant—as a lawyer, Preston Van Sant was very meticulous. Randomly capitalizing words without intent wasn't in his nature. John shook his head, his mind foggy from lack of food and sleep. He drifted off...

He was jolted awake by Derik yanking at the rope that bound him to the bunk.

"Wha...What are you doing."

Derik bound John's legs, allowing just enough slack so he would be able to shuffle along. Then, he tied his hands behind his back.

"Come on, you're going to your new room for a while."

"Why?"

Derik didn't answer but guided John to the door and pushed him through. John stopped and looked down the valley. With a clear view, he immediately recognized the terrain below. In the distance, at the foot of the valley, was the Lowe River, the trail, and beyond it, Robe Lake. He stared hard, realizing that the boarding house should be visible, but couldn't make it out. At least he now knew where he was—*Sulphide Gulch*—not that it did him any good at the moment.

Derik shoved him, then turned him uphill. They moved slowly, John stumbling several times until they reached the opening to the adit. John stiffened and resisted. Derik shoved him, and he fell to his knees.

"Get up and get in there."

"I'm not going in that hole."

Derik pulled the Colt .45 from the holster and leveled it at his head.

"You won't shoot me—you need me."

"Do I? You've already said you don't know what the clue means, so I have to look elsewhere. I don't want to shoot you, but you better cooperate."

John sneered at him as he struggled to get up.

"Don't forget—I can still pay Stella a visit."

John made it to his feet and took a step toward the entrance. "Don't."

"Then move on."

John reached the portal and looked inside. It was dark, with a flickering, yellow glow in the distance. The opening was framed in timber to prevent collapse. Just inside were two wooden boxes stacked against the rock wall with a piece of tin covering. Beyond the boxes was a pile of rusting drill steel, four or five feet long, and a wooden crate of bits. He paused to look further, but Derik shoved him forward.

"Why are you taking me here?"

"Not that it's any of your concern, but I'm going to town to get some supplies. If anyone happens upon the cabin, they won't find you there. Keep moving."

"You don't have to put me in here. What reason would anyone have for coming up to the cabin?"

"You never know who might be out and about," said Derik.

John could only hope someone was out looking for him, but the time it took for them to reach the hiding spot made him doubtful. With the river crossing, it was clear they were off the beaten path.

"Move on," said Derik, shoving further into the adit.

Water dripped from overhead in places, at times puddling to several inches on the adit floor. John tried to straddle the rails to keep his feet dry, but they were too far apart and the rope binding his legs too short. He kept slipping off, nearly falling several times.

After what John judged to be about a hundred and fifty feet, they reached the lantern, hung from a twenty penny spike driven into a crack in the rock wall. Next to the lantern was an empty ore car, a rusting hulk that had slipped off the rails and was now a permanent fixture.

"Stop here," said Derik. "Sit."

John leaned his back against the ore car and slid down to a sitting position.

"See the nice dry spot I picked out for you?" said Derik as he proceeded to lash John to the ore car. "You'll be nice and comfortable here while I'm gone."

John shivered. Though it was nearly sixty degrees outside, the mine hovered near forty. "I'm going to freeze to death in here."

"Wait here, I'll be back," said Derik. He took a couple of steps, turned and looked at John, laughed, then continued on.

The veins on John's forehead bulged as the rage and contempt he felt for the man built. *He thinks he's so blasted funny.*

He surveyed his surroundings—there was a timber set not far from the ore car. He hoped it would prevent the whole thing from caving in on him. He could see small veins of minerals reflecting in the dim light. Whatever it was, it must not have been enough to warrant mining. He couldn't tell how much further in the adit went, but looking the other way, he realized the entrance wasn't visible. The adit took a slight bend at one point, such that you couldn't see the exit. Struggling along in the dark and trying not to fall, he hadn't noticed.

After several minutes, he heard Derik returning. He waited, and when he came into view, he was carrying a couple of blankets and a canteen.

"Here you go," he said as he covered John up. "Wouldn't want my favorite prisoner getting cold now, would I."

He took the cap off the canteen and poured a dribble over John, allowing him to get a drink.

"I'm hungry," said John.

"You'll get something when I return."

"Aren't you afraid someone will recognize you?"

"Not really. I've got a plan. The best part is, the two looking for me have never seen me, and your friend Thomas is out of commission—probably dead. So that leaves Stella as the only one who can identify me."

"There are others in town—the hotel clerk, storekeepers—you'll be recognized."

Derik turned and headed for the entrance. "Don't worry about it. You've got enough trouble," he shouted as he disappeared from view.

† † †

Jack drove the wagon around to the back of his office and pulled the handbrake. Thomas, seated next to him, jumped down and, with one hand, wrapped the reins around the hitching post.

"Do you think you can ride with only one good arm?" said Jack.

"I can manage."

"I've got saddles in the shed back here, and the other horse is there," said Jack, pointing to a small fenced area just beyond the shed.

The plan was to leave the wagon and for each of them to ride a horse, allowing faster travel and easier maneuvering should the need arise. They knew there were two horses used by Van Sant—if they found John, he'd have a horse.

"Where do we start?" said Sdzeè as she finished cinching the saddle on Jack's other horse.

"I'm in tight with the fellows down at the docks. I'll start there and see if I can turn up anything. You and Thomas check the shops and the hotel. Thomas can describe him pretty well, so maybe we'll get lucky," said Jack.

"Sounds reasonable," said Thomas.

"Oh, and Sdzeè, keep an eye on that one-winged husband of yours. He has a penchant for getting in trouble."

Sdzeè laughed. "I know. I can not take him anywhere."

"Alright, that's enough," said Thomas. "We've got a serious task ahead of us."

Jack mounted up and pointed his horse toward the docks. "Let's meet back here in a couple of hours."

"Will do," said Thomas as he managed to pull himself up into the saddle without his left arm.

They parted, Sdzeè and Thomas heading first for the hotel. The clerk recognized the description of Derik but hadn't seen him since he checked out. However, he did offer a suggestion—Derik spent a lot of time in the saloon—someone there might know something.

Thomas remembered the woman at the saloon who had pointed him to Goat Creek in the first place. *Was there a chance Derik had returned for another visit?* It was worth a look.

They arrived at the Bohemian Saloon, and though early in the day, it sounded like there were plenty of customers inside.

"You should wait with the horses, Sdzeè."

She laughed. "If you think I am letting you go in alone, Thomas Thornton, you are wrong."

"But—"

"I am going in."

Thomas shrugged his shoulders and pushed the door open for her with his good arm. The place hadn't changed—stale beer, cigars, and men. Sdzeè garnered plenty of stares from the drunks, but they said nothing. Along the back wall, Thomas spied the young blonde he talked to the last time. He headed her way.

"You back for more?" she said.

"Have you seen Derik since we last talked?"

"Look at me—you know what I have isn't free—what's it worth to you?"

Thomas sighed. "Look—a man's life is at stake. How about a little common decency."

She laughed out loud at him as Sdzeè stepped closer. "Decent—that word is rarely used about me. Who's this? Your guide?"

"She's my wife. Now, will you help us?"

She crossed her arms and stared at them, then relaxed. "Humph—wife. Okay, what do you want."

Have you seen him?"

She looked toward the door, then down the bar. "He

was here an hour or so ago. He snuck in the back and had me buy a bottle for him."

Thomas looked at her intently. "Did he say where he was going? Where he was staying?"

"What happened to your arm?" she said.

"Never mind that. Do you know?"

"No, just that he was in town to get supplies and head back up."

"Back up? What does that mean?"

"How would I know? I didn't ask. I learned long ago not to ask too many questions."

"Is there anything else you can tell us?"

She shook her head. "Not that I can think of."

Thomas nodded. "Thanks for the information. What's your name, by the way?" said Thomas.

"Destiny—just like my hometown."

Thomas shot a glance at Sdzeè. "Your hometown?"

"Yes," said Destiny. "Tacoma."

† † †

Derik rode the horse to the back of the general store and tied her off. He looked around, and seeing no one, made his way carefully to the front. A quick look up and down the street revealed no one nearby—at least no one that would care to notice him. He pulled his hat down low, stepped up on the boardwalk, and entered the store.

Hemple and Dougherty Pioneer Outfitters sat on the edge of town, the perfect place for Derik to purchase what he needed. He'd never been inside their establishment, having done what little provisioning before at the *A.J. Fish & Co.* store. He was pretty certain no one would recognize him, especially since there were few customers in the store.

He handed the list to the clerk who set about fetching the items—a slab of bacon, hardtack, five pounds of potatoes, powdered eggs, and an ax. She placed each item on the counter as she fetched them from the shelves and bins.

"Anything else?"

Derik shook his head, then paused. "Wait—I need something to cook in, and some lard."

She nodded and returned with a cast-iron skillet. "This do?"

"That's good, and that'll do it."

The clerk put the groceries in a burlap bag and wrote out the receipt. Derik foolishly thought about walking out without paying but only for an instant. He dug into his pocket and grudgingly slapped the cash down on the counter. The clerk stepped back and stared at him.

"Do I know you?" she said.

Derik picked up the bag, ax, and skillet. "Don't think so."

"You look familiar. Ah—I've got it—you stayed at the Valdez Hotel recently. I work there as a maid part-time."

Derik shook his head.

"I'm sure of it. Let's see...your name is...Mr. Lowe—yes, that's it."

"Oh, right. That must be where you saw me," he said as he turned to leave, thankful that he'd used the alias while staying in town.

"Have a good day, Mr. Lowe," she said as he stepped out into the noonday sun.

† † †

Thomas and Sdzeè left *A.J. Fish & Co.* and untied

their horses from the hitching post. After Destiny told them Van Sant was in town for supplies, they decided to check the stores that sold groceries, assuming that would be the main thing he'd need—apart from the booze.

They'd already been to the *City Market* as well. In addition to providing Van Sant's name, Thomas gave a detailed description of him—in case he was using an alias. The clerk at Fish & Co. thought he sounded familiar but hadn't seen him recently.

They mounted up and, riding side by side, headed to their last stop, Hemple and Dougherty's.

"We are running out of places to look," said Sdzeè.

"We barely missed him at the saloon. Our only hope is he's still in town."

They turned the corner, and Sdzeè grabbed his arm. He pulled up on the reins. "What—"

"Shush," said Sdzeè. "Look at the man that just rode out from the back of the store. He sounds like your description of Van Sant."

Thomas strained to look, shading his eyes from the sun with his hand. The man was riding away from them. "I can't tell. It could be."

"We should move closer."

"If it's him, I don't want to be seen."

The man reached the end of the street, and as he turned onto the trail leading out of town, Thomas caught a look at his face—and a broad mustache.

"That's him. I'm sure of it."

"We need to follow him," said Sdzeè. "But not be seen."

"If he sees me, he'll bolt—or start shooting. We could catch him, but he may not tell us where John is. We're better off following him to his hideout."

"I have an idea, Thomas. He does not know me by sight. It was too dark when we passed him on the Goat Creek trail. I will follow as far back as possible, and you follow me, keeping your distance."

"That might work."

"It is the best chance we have."

"What about Jack. We're supposed to meet him about now."

"We can not wait. We must follow."

CHAPTER 21

Sdzeè followed Van Sant, careful to stay far enough behind to not arouse suspicion. He seemed to not be in a hurry as he meandered along the trail leading out of town. Since Stella saw no one go by as she sat on the porch the night Van Sant was on the move, he had to turn off somewhere between town and the boarding house.

Thomas slowed down a bit—he was closer to Sdzeè than was safe. He looked at his watch. They'd been following Van Sant for just over forty minutes. Five minutes later, Sdzeè stopped on the trail. Thomas stopped and waited. After several minutes, Sdzeè motioned for him to join her. He didn't move and, she signaled again, more insistently. Finally, he nudged the horse forward but not too fast.

"He turned off just ahead," said Sdzeè quietly.

"Which way?"

"To the right, toward the river."

"Let's move up—slowly."

They walked the horses ahead, staring off into the woods along the trail in case Van Sant was near. Reaching the point where he turned, they stopped and looked toward the river but couldn't see him. His path through the trees was pretty obvious, the grass was trampled down, and in spots, tracks were visible in the mud. They de-

211

cided to follow.

Now that they were off the trail, if Van Sant spotted either of them, the game would be up. Travelers on the Valdez-Eagle trail were one thing—people following others through the woods, another. Sdzeè and Thomas dismounted and led the horses. They moved slowly, hoping to avoid being seen. The sound of the river grew louder as they reached a thick stand of spruce.

"I think he is going to cross the river," said Sdzeè.

"Let's leave the horses here and take a peek."

They tied off the horses to a spruce tree, crouched down, and made their way through the trees to where they could just see the river. Sdzeè was right—Van Sant was halfway across the river, stopped on a small gravel bar in the middle of the braided channels. He turned his horse toward their direction—they immediately hit the ground and lay in the grass. Van Sant stared their way for what seemed like a long time, then turned and continued, pushing forward into the river.

"Now what?" said Sdzeè.

Thomas looked at the path behind him. The dirt was soft in places, making it possible to track Van Sant as long as he didn't get onto hard ground. Still, there was a risk they would lose him.

"We should have Jack with us. You are not ready for a fight with only one arm," said Sdzeè.

"I'll keep tracking him from a distance. Now that he's bushwacking, it should be easy for me to remain unseen. You ride as fast as you can to meet Jack, gather up what you think we'll need, and then return."

"How will I find you?"

Thomas pulled the hunting knife from its sheath and held it up. "I'll put a small blaze mark on the trees every so often for you to follow. Once I figure out his final destination, I'll hold up until you and Jack arrive."

"I am not sure of this plan."

"I'll be fine. I'm not going to confront Van Sant—now hurry."

They returned to the horses, unhitched them, and mounted up. "Be careful, Thomas Thornton," said Sdzeè as she turned and booted the horse in the ribs.

Thomas watched as the horse galloped away, then turned toward the river. He looked carefully along the far bank—Van Sant was not in sight. It was a risk to cross the river in the open—he could easily be seen if Van Sant chose to stop and look back from the trees.

The water came up quickly, soaking his boots as the horse lunged forward. For a moment, he thought she would lose her footing, and they'd end up downriver, but she made it to the gravel bar in the middle. Thomas patted her neck. "Good job, girl."

He continued across, then moved upriver until he found where Van Sant headed into the trees. He paused to listen, but couldn't hear anything above the sound of the river, so he headed into the trees—slowly.

Van Sant's trail was easy to follow—the grass was knocked down, and the horse tracks showed up well. Thomas stopped and cut the bark from the tree next to him without dismounting, then continued following. Every hundred feet or so, he stopped and listened, then added another blaze mark.

He finally reached the old mining trail that came up from the river. He stopped and checked the tracks. Satisfied that Van Sant had continued on and not turned toward the river, he blazed trees on both sides of the trail before continuing.

From the gait of the tracks, he could tell Van Sant was moving slow. He stopped and waited a few minutes, fearful that he was pushing ahead faster and would overtake him. He wanted a cigarette but didn't dare risk it. *Where in the world is he headed?*

The urge to overtake him and force him to tell where John was became nearly overwhelming, but he knew it was foolish. Van Sant might just as well shoot him dead than tell him. Thomas rubbed his left arm—a reminder of precisely what kind of man they were dealing with.

† † †

Sdzeè galloped up to *Jack's Freight and Draying* and hopped off the horse, barely taking time to hitch it to the rail. She bounded up the steps and flung open the door to find the office empty. She returned outside and looked up and down the street. It was past the agreed rendezvous time—he must have returned and found her and Thomas not there and left again.

She unhitched the horse and swung up into the saddle, unsure of where to look. Finally, she decided to head toward the docks since that was where he was to start his search. She passed the *St. Elias* hotel and was about to turn toward the docks when she heard her name.

"Sdzeè, over here."

It was Jack—she had ridden right past him as he was coming out of a side street.

"Where's Thomas?" he said as he joined her.

She explained what was going on and the need to hurry. "I am worried that Thomas will take matters into his own hands against that ch'inee'iin."

"Sorry—what?"

"Van Sant is a ch'inee'iin—thief."

"Ah—where is he going? Do you know?"

"No, only he crossed the river and headed into the woods. Thomas is blazing trees for us to follow."

"Ah. We'll need to take a few provisions in case we get stuck overnight."

Sdzeè nodded. "We must hurry, though."

"I have everything we need at the office, so let's stop there and then head out."

"I just hope Thomas waits for us," said Sdzeè as she whipped the reins across the backside of her horse and galloped for the office.

Derik returned to the cabin by midafternoon. He dismounted, tied the horse off where it could graze on the alpine grass, and unloaded the supplies. He was hungry, but there was no wood for the stove. Being above timberline had certain disadvantages. He went back to the horse, loosed her, and rode downhill. It was some distance down the gulch to timberline where he could chop off enough dead branches to get a meager fire going.

A half-hour later, he was back at the cabin with a bundle of dead spruce limbs lashed to the saddle. The gnarly branches weren't easy to deal with, and the horse wasn't happy having them rubbing against her, the remnants of needles jabbing her as she walked. He secured the horse and carried the bundle into the cabin. Within minutes there was a fire blazing in the rusty stove. The bad thing about dead spruce was it burned too quickly. He looked at the pile of branches, the largest no more than two inches in diameter, and wondered how long they would last.

While the stove heated up, he left the cabin and trudged uphill to the adit to fetch John. He reached the entrance and started in, only to find it was pitch black. The lantern had gone out.

"Devil it!" said Derik as he hauled off and kicked the stack of boxes just inside the adit. The tin covering clattered to the ground, echoing through the adit. He looked inside the top box and found a couple of hammers, four used candles, and three carbide lamps. He picked up one of the lamps but couldn't figure out how to use it. He cursed and sat the box aside.

The other box contained two more carbide lamps, a tin of carbide, and—a lantern. Derik picked it up and shook it, hoping to hear the sound of fuel sloshing inside. It sounded like there was something in it, so he removed the glass globe and turned up the wick. He pulled out a match from his pocket and struck it, then held it against the wick. It flickered for a second, then went out. He cursed again, shook the lantern, and tried again. This time it lit, smoke rising as he replaced the globe and adjusted the wick downward.

Armed with the lantern, he made his way to the ore car and found John half-conscious under the two blankets. It wasn't the smartest thing to do—leaving him in those temperatures for so long. *Maybe he'll be more willing to cooperate now.*

Derik hauled back and kicked his boot, rousing him.

"Wha—"

"Get up. I have a fire going in the cabin."

John threw off the blankets and struggled to stand. His legs were stiff from the cold and damp, and Derik finally had to help him to his feet. He untied him, took the lantern from the hook, and led John to the entrance.

By the time they reached the cabin, John's legs were working well enough for him to walk without help. Derik reached around him and opened the door, then pushed him forward into the warmth. John stumbled to the bunk and sat down without being told. Derik smiled and secured him, then sat the lanterns on the shelf. He stuffed two branches into the stove, then sat on the bench.

"How are you feeling now? Feeling like talking about that clue—that riddle?"

John shrugged, the feeling returning to his extremities as the stove radiated heat throughout the tiny space. "I've told you. I don't know what it means."

Derik huffed. "That's unfortunate. I was going to feed you, but now I'm not so sure."

"You shot the only person that knows what it means," said John, lying.

"Well, then, let's hope for your sake he's still alive."

† † †

Thomas followed the mining trail nearly to Washbowl Basin, where it took a sharp turn right up a narrow, steep-sided valley. It became clear that Van Sant was headed up Sulphide Gulch, one of the valleys visible from Stella's front porch. He remembered relaxing on the porch—it seemed ages ago now—drinking morning coffee as Stella rattled off the names of the valleys and mountain peaks that graced their view.

He could follow on, but there was only one way in and out of the valley. From the head of the valley, the only way to travel further would require Van Sant to trek over one or more glaciers—something Thomas was pretty sure he wouldn't do on horseback. *There must be a hiding place up there.*

He had a decision to make—continue or wait for Stella and Jack. He decided on the latter, placed a final blaze mark on a nearby tree, and made his way off the narrow mining trail into a meadow fifty yards away. This would give him cover if Van Sant returned, but he could also see when Sdzeè and Jack arrived. He tied off the horse and sat under a large spruce tree, his back to the trunk. Deciding to risk it, Thomas rolled a cigarette and lit up. His arm was throbbing from the ride, and he was hungry. No longer moving, a chill set in. He pulled his coat tight and, though he fought it, drifted off.

He awoke to the sound of the horse straining against the lead and rearing on her hind legs. She was snorting, ears laid back, and distressed. He stood and looked around but saw nothing. "What do you smell, old girl?" he said as he patted her neck, trying to calm her. He pulled the .44-40 carbine from the scabbard, even though it would be difficult to aim at anything with only one good arm.

A loud snap in the brush twenty yards distant caused the hair on the back of his neck to stand up. He moved to the left a bit and could see a large brown patch of fur moving between the trees. He backed up and sat down, his back against the tree and knees raised. He shouldered the carbine and placed the barrel on one knee, knowing it would be difficult to aim and chamber another round without his left arm. He removed the .45 Peacemaker from its holster, placed it beside him on his right side, and then waited.

The figure emerged from the trees into the meadow thirty yards away. It was a large grizzly—from the size, Thomas guessed it was a boar. The horse was whirling around, struggling to get free. The grizzly sniffed the air, head held high, then stood on its hind legs. Thomas tried to aim the carbine at the center of the bear's chest, but with one arm, it proved difficult.

The bear returned to all fours and circled the edge of

the meadow, trying to catch the wind. Thomas shifted against the tree, trying to maintain his aim. The bear stopped again and raised up, sniffing. He thought about firing a shot to ward it off, but that could alert Van Sant. The bear went back on all fours and was swaying back and forth, popping its jaws.

Thomas knew that was a warning sign—he had to be ready in case the bear charged. A loud noise from the other side of the meadow caught his attention. He was afraid to take his eyes off the bear but feared he was surrounded. He shot a glance and saw Jack and Sdzeè thundering toward the meadow at full tilt. The grizzly turned, stood on its hind legs for a second, decided it was outnumbered, and bolted back into the brush.

Thomas lowered the carbine and slumped against the tree. Jack and Sdzeè reined in their horses and jumped off, Sdzeè with the .45-70 in her hands.

"Are you alright?" she said.

Thomas managed a weak grin. "Yes, now that you're here—wasn't sure how I would manage if it came to a showdown."

Jack gave him a hand and helped him to his feet. Thomas turned to his horse and stroked her neck, trying to calm her. "Easy girl."

"Looks like we got here just in time," said Jack.

"Yes, it was going to get ugly if that grizzly charged—I was afraid if I fired, it would alert Van Sant."

"Do you think it will come back?" said Sdzeè.

Jack shook his head. "I doubt it. He was moving pretty fast when he turned tail. Now, where is Van Sant?"

"I followed his trail until he turned up the valley. There's no way out without going into the ice field, I think."

"Do you think he knows you were following?"

"No, I never actually caught sight of him, just tracked him to here."

"What is our plan?" said Sdzeè.

Jack looked at his pocket watch. "Well, it's close to three p.m. now. We can follow, but we risk chasing him in the dark."

"I think we need to press on. The longer Van Sant has John, the more danger he is in," said Thomas.

"I wonder how far up the valley he went?" said Sdzeè.

"No idea," said Thomas.

"The valley is nearly four miles long. There is an abandoned mine and a small cabin about two miles up—nothing else beyond that," said Jack.

"That must be where he's hiding out," said Thomas. "Can we get close without being seen?"

"I doubt it, said Jack. "I took a pack train up there years ago when the mine was active, and it's above tree-line—minimal cover except for low scrub brush."

"So you know this area," said Sdzeè.

"Yes, I suspected that's where Van Sant was headed when we got to the old mining trail."

"How do we proceed?" said Thomas. "Seems it's going to be hard sneaking up on him—we'll be an easy target as we come up the valley."

"We could take the horses to near timberline, wait until dark, then go in on foot. I remember about where the cabin becomes visible on the way up," said Jack.

"It might be pretty dark unless the weather breaks," said Thomas. "Some moonlight would help."

Jack nodded. "It's either go under cover of darkness or a straight in, frontal assault."

"Neither sounds appealing, but I say we go now," said

Thomas.

"We have one thing going for us," said Jack.

"What's that?"

"Last I saw, the cabin had no windows."

CHAPTER 22

John juggled the tin plate on his lap as he gulped down the fried potatoes, eggs, and bacon. He hadn't eaten in what seemed like days. It was a challenge, eating one-handed with the other lashed to the bunk, but he managed.

Van Sant already ate—he was leaning against the wall smoking a cigarette.

"Feeling better? Ready to talk?"

John scraped the last of the eggs from the plate and downed them. "What do you want to talk about?"

"The clue, of course."

John sighed. "I can't make it any clearer. It's a mystery to me. If anyone could understand it, it should be you—your father wrote it."

"You knew my father—you knew he had little to do with me from the time I was fourteen—from the time he divorced my mother."

"So why did he tell you about the money?"

"I think it was guilt. Guilt for abandoning me."

"From what I saw of him toward the end, I don't think he was capable of having a true emotion. But blood is blood."

"It doesn't matter why. I've been scraping in the dirt for every penny—that's going to change."

"I don't care about the money anymore. I'm happy here with my life," said John.

Van Sant laughed. "I don't believe you. No one in their right mind would give up a small fortune."

"It's true. Let me go, and I will do all I can to help you."

"Not likely. You or your friend will tell me what I want to know."

"Let me see the letter from your father—maybe it has a clue you haven't noticed," said John.

Van Sant huffed. "I'm not stupid."

"I didn't say you were. Another set of eyes wouldn't hurt."

Van Sant tossed the cigarette stub on the dirt floor and crushed it out. He stared at John, then pulled out the letter from his vest pocket. "Here, but if you tear it up, you're a dead man."

"I'm not going to damage it, just read it," said John as he unfolded it.

It was from Preston, dated over two years ago:

```
Derik,

I know I haven't always been there for you.  My
Destiny was elsewhere.  I'm embarking on a trip
to Alaska to tie up a loose end.

I have acquired a large sum of money through a
deceitful but justified act.  John Palmer and his
brat daughter will try to get it back, thus
necessitating my journey.

In the event I do not return, you will find a
clue to the money sewn into my clothes.

I could just tell you, but alas, I do not trust
you fully.  If I am killed, you'll have to work
for the fortune.  I believe you are smart enough
to decipher the clue and, as the horrific father
you think I am, this is the last appalling thing
I can do.
```

John seethed at the mention of his daughter but hid it. He handed the letter back to Van Sant. "That's quite a letter—a spiteful, malicious man to the end. I see he didn't sign it."

Van Sant folded the letter and returned it to his pocket. "I guess he couldn't figure out how to sign it—certainly not with love—I don't think he ever felt that way toward me."

"I'm sorry."

Van Sant growled, repulsed by his show of vulnerability. "I don't need your pity. You've seen the letter—tell me what the clue means."

"Give me a minute," said John as he thought about the letter. *Curious, that word destiny again, and capitalized*, he thought to himself. He didn't know what it meant, or even if it was significant, but he wasn't going to mention it to Van Sant.

"Well?"

"I see nothing in there that helps," said John.

"That's what I told you."

"Now what? I don't know where the money is or how to help you. Let me go—all of us will keep quiet. You can continue your search."

"I might do that if I believed you. That's the advantage of having a liar and a scoundrel for a father—you don't take anything at face value."

"Your father was good at hiding his true nature. I never suspected anything until he turned on me."

Van Sant said nothing, put on his coat, and picked up the rifle he'd left by the door.

"Where are you going?"

"You say I shot the only person who can decipher the clue. I'm going to find him."

"Wait!" shouted John.

Too late—the door slammed—Van Sant was gone.

† † †

The horses were tied just below timberline, out of sight. The narrow creek that flowed down the valley was lined with low brush, providing a small element of cover. From their vantage point, the cabin wasn't visible.

"I say we work our way up the creek, using the brush to hide our approach," said Jack.

"I think that's the best bet—we'll be too in the open otherwise," said Thomas.

"What happens when we get near the cabin?" said Sdzeè. "If we call out, Van Sant may harm John before we can get to him—if he's even there."

"I don't like the way that sounds, but in that case, I say we break the door down and go in with guns leveled," said Thomas.

Sdzeè rested the .45-70 on her shoulder and shook her head. "You may have trouble in that regard."

"I can still handle a revolver, even though the carbine gave me trouble when the bear was sniffing around."

"Let's hope there's no gunfire," said Jack. "If we can get John out of there, we'll let someone else deal with Van Sant."

Thomas nodded. "As much as I despise him, I don't want to see another dead Van Sant."

"How far is it to the cabin?" said Sdzeè.

"A little over a mile, I reckon," said Jack. "All up-hill."

"Let's get moving. I don't want to do this in the dark," said Thomas.

Jack nodded and took the lead, walking along the edge of the water. The narrow creek was not more than a foot or so deep in most places. For the most part, they could avoid the water, but in a few places, to stay within the cover of the brush on the bank, they had to step from boulder to boulder.

It wasn't long before the cabin came into view in the distance. They stopped, hunkered down, and listened. Hearing nothing, they proceeded slower, keeping their heads down. Finally, fifty yards from the cabin, Jack raised his hand, signaling a stop. The door was closed—they listened, straining to hear above the bubbling of the little creek.

"I think I hear talking," said Sdzeè, her voice low.

"That's a good sign," said Thomas.

"Two horses tied up beyond. That means he's still here," said Thomas. "Let's move in."

They stepped up on the low bank of the creek and started toward the cabin. Suddenly the door swung open, and Van Sant stepped out. They heard a yell from inside as the door slammed shut. Van Sant turned toward the creek, spotted them, and shouldered his rifle.

"Put it down," yelled Thomas. "You're outnumbered. All we want is John."

Van Sant fired a shot that whizzed just over their heads. The sound of the lever being worked echoed in their ears as he chambered another round.

"Take cover," yelled Jack.

The trio retreated to the creek, the bank providing just enough concealment. Another round hit the ground twenty feet from the creek, then the sound of Van Sant running. Thomas peered over the bank and saw him, headed for the horses.

"He's headed for his horse," said Thomas.

Sdzeè stood and put two rounds from the .45-70 near the horses, careful not to hit them. Van Sant turned and fired off a single ill-placed round, then headed uphill for the cover of the mine.

Jack and Thomas left the cover of the creek and ran to the cabin, Sdzeè covering them with the .45-70 in case Van Sant started shooting. As near as she could tell, Van Sant disappeared into the mine. She moved quickly past the cabin to just below the mine dump, knelt, and kept the .45-70 pointed at the entrance.

"You alright there, Sdzeè?" yelled Thomas.

"I am fine. Find John. I will keep the ch'inee'iin at bay."

Thomas was the first to enter the cabin, with Jack close behind.

"Thomas!"

"Are you alright, John?"

"Yes, untie me."

Thomas and Jack worked quickly to untie him, then helped him stand.

"Can you walk?"

"I'll make it—just need to get my legs working again."

A gunshot echoed from outside, and the group rushed out. Sdzeè was ducked down against the mine dump—Van Sant was not in sight.

"What happened?" said Thomas as they joined her.

"He popped out for a second and took a shot. Didn't get near me," said Sdzeè. "It is good to see you, John."

"Glad to be free."

"Have you been in there—what's in the mine?" said Jack.

"I've been in part way. He left me tied up to an ore car while he went to town. I didn't see much, other than some boxes of old equipment at the entrance."

"Well, there's no way he's getting past us," said Thomas.

"Maybe he thinks we will go away," said Sdzeè.

"Well, he's wrong. He's going to pay for what he did."

"Is there light in there?"

John shook his head. "No, both the lanterns I know about are in the cabin, and they're out of fuel. So, unless he grabbed something from the boxes at the entrance, he's in the dark."

"One way to find out," said Jack. "Let's move in."

CHAPTER 23

Working their way along the slope so Van Sant wouldn't be able to spot them, Jack and Thomas reached the entrance to the mine. John, still weak from his ordeal, took up a guard position with Sdzeè further back.

The tin sheet lay on the ground next to the wooden boxes. Jack carefully poked his head around to take a quick look. There were a couple of candles, carbide lamps, and other mining tools. Jack peered into the darkness from the edge of the opening, careful not to stick his head out too far. In the distance, he could see a dim, flickering reflection off the side of the adit. He retreated.

"I think he's got a candle in there—pretty dim."

"Can you see him?" said Thomas.

"No, I think he must be around a bend in the workings. All I could see was the light bouncing off the wall."

"The workings take a turn before the ore car. That must be where he is," said John.

"Probably using the ore car for cover," said Thomas. "I don't relish going in there in the dark."

"We can use carbide lamps. There's several in the box and a tin of carbide," said Jack.

Thomas shook his head. "If we do that, he'll know we're coming."

Jack nodded. "That's the risk—let's see if we can talk

231

him out before we decide to go in."

Thomas moved closer to the entrance and yelled, "Come on out, Van Sant. It's over—you can't stay in there forever."

No answer. Thomas backed away and spoke to John in a low voice, "Is it possible he's stashed supplies in there?"

"I didn't see any, and he hasn't had a chance to since he returned. If there's supplies in there, he stashed them before he dragged me up."

"So he probably can't stay in there very long," said Jack.

"Plenty of water dripping in there, but the temperature is unpleasant. I'd guess barely forty degrees, if that," said John. "I nearly froze when he had me tied up in there."

"Let's try something else," said Thomas as he started for the entrance.

"What do you have in mind?" said Jack.

"A threat. Maybe that will bring him out."

Thomas approached and peered carefully into the mine. "Come out, Van Sant, or we'll tie our horses to these timbers and bring the whole thing down. Then you can stay in there forever."

He listened but heard nothing. It was dark, and the only sound was the dripping of water from the cracks in the roof of the workings. He turned to Jack. "It's dark in there—no sign of light."

Jack took a look. "You're right. He must have moved further in or put out his candle."

"I thought your threat would get a response. Being trapped in a mine ought to put the fear in anyone," said John.

Thomas tried again. "This is your last chance, or we're pulling the timbers!"

Again—nothing—just the dripping of water in the darkness.

"He is not coming out," said Sdzeè. "Stubborn ch'inee'iin."

Thomas picked up a carbide lamp and handed it to Jack, then grabbed the tin of carbide. "Help me get this lit—I'm going in."

Jack unscrewed the bottom of the lamp and sat it down, then took the carbide can and pried the lid off with his knife. "I hope this stuff is dry or, we'll be using candles."

"Would not a lantern from the cabin be better—if we can find fuel?" said Sdzeè.

"See the reflector on these?" said Thomas holding up a second lamp. "They focus the light a bit, helping us to see further, plus it's not in your eyes like when you're holding a lantern."

"Carbide looks good," said Jack as he dropped a handful of the pea-sized chunks of carbide into the bottom of the lamp and screwed the top back on. "All we need now is water."

He popped the cap from the top of the lamp, shut the regulator lever, and handed it to Thomas. "Fill the reservoir with water from one of those drips."

Thomas nodded and held the lamp under a stream of water until it was full, then snapped the cap shut. He handed it back to Jack. "I can't light it with one hand."

Jack turned the lever a couple of clicks, held his hand over the reflector to let the gas build, then swiped his hand quickly across the striker wheel. The flint sparked, the lamp made a whoosh sound and lit. He adjusted the lever until the flame was about a half-inch long, then handed the lamp to Thomas. "You sure you can handle this with one hand? Maybe you should wait outside."

Thomas shook his head vigorously. "I can hold the lamp in my left and still have my revolver in the right."

Jack nodded and readied the other lamp, then replaced the lid on the tin of carbide. He filled the reservoir and lit the lamp. "Ready, set?"

Thomas nodded. "Let's stick to the left side."

They entered the adit, the yellow glow of the carbide lamps reflecting off the wet roof and walls of the workings. They waited, hoping Van Sant wasn't lying in wait. Satisfied, they moved forward slowly. Sdzeè and John moved up to the entrance and took up position on both sides. "Be careful," she whispered as they disappeared into the damp darkness.

† † †

Derik cursed as the splash of water from the ceiling hit the candle and put it out. There was barely a hint of light visible from the entrance around the bend in the adit—not enough to distinguish anything around him.

The threats from the entrance didn't scare him, and he smiled as he remained silent. Forcing them to enter gave him the upper hand. He crouched behind the ore car, pulled out one of the few matches remaining, and was about to strike it against the rusty metal surface when he stopped. Lighting the candle would give him away. He shoved the match back into his pocket and listened.

Voices came as muffled echoes, suppressed by the dampness of the adit. Derik heard Thomas clearly when he yelled but couldn't make out what they were saying among themselves. One thing seemed clear—Thornton was alive and well. He still held out hope that one of them held the answer to his father's cryptic clue. For that, he needed both Palmer and Thornton alive—whoever else with them was just in the way.

He didn't have a plan—entering the mine was a spur of the moment decision to get out of the line of fire. Had he reached the horses, they probably would have shot him before he got ten feet.

Getting trapped in the mine wasn't going to happen. Somehow, he had to get the upper hand. If he could deal with them one at a time, it would work. *I've come too far to let them get the best of me,* he thought as he leaned against the ore car, the Colt .45 resting on his knee—ready.

The lights—a pair of them—flickered around the corner and, bit by bit, grew brighter. Derik wished he'd explored the mine more fully. Perhaps there was another entrance by which he could escape. He knew little of mining but did know that sometimes mines had multiple levels, some with an entry to the outside. He couldn't recall seeing an adit on the slope above this one, but that didn't mean it wasn't there. He was conflicted—wait here and try to get the upper hand, or go deeper in the mine, looking for a way out.

The lights were now accompanied by the sound of footsteps. It was decision time—if he was going to move, he needed to do it before his pursuers came into sight. He stood slowly and turned, looked back once, then moved deeper into the mine, feeling his way along the wall, hoping he wouldn't trip over something.

The lights were now far behind him. He kept his back to them and lit the candle. Ahead of him was a fork in the mine workings. The main one with the rails continued straight ahead, while to the right, another opening split off at a slight angle. He wondered why the miners would do such a thing, ignorant of the quartz vein over his head. He smiled, pulled the other candle from his pocket, lit it, then blew out the first one. He tossed it eight feet down the opening to the right, then continued straight ahead. He smiled. *That'll buy me some time.*

† † †

Jack and Thomas continued until they reached the bend in the workings. They stopped and listened, then Thomas moved forward just enough to see down the adit. Aiming the carbide lamp, he panned it around until it illuminated the ore car.

"There's the ore car."

Jack moved forward and took a look. "I don't see Van Sant, do you?"

"No, but he could be hiding just beyond. I'm going to move up—cover me."

Jack nodded and watched Thomas inch forward, crouching down to present a smaller target. Ten feet from the ore car, he could tell Van Sant wasn't there. He motioned for Jack to move up, and he joined him.

"He's gone further in," said Thomas.

"Appears so. Look, he left his rifle," said Jack.

Thomas looked and saw the rifle laying between the ore car and the rock wall of the adit. "That means he only has a revolver," he said, knowing full well that Van Sant's revolver was enough of a threat by itself.

The pair continued forward, vigilant in case Van Sant was lying in ambush. Finally, they reached the split in the drift.

"Which way?" said Thomas.

Jack looked down the opening on the right as far as his light allowed. He did the same down the main drift.

"Not—"

"What is it?"

Jack took another few steps, bent over, and picked up a burned-out candle. He held it up to Thomas. "The wax is still a tiny bit warm."

"Now we know which way he went," said Thomas as he moved past Jack and stared down the side drift. "Follow me."

† † †

Derik reached the end of the main drift. Through the dim light of the candle, he could see a ladder extending up through a small diameter shaft of bare, jagged rock. He couldn't see the top, but a gentle breeze of fresh air was flowing from above.

The wooden ladder was dripping with water from above. Derik put his weight on the lower rung—it held. He took another step up—the ladder creaked but held. With both hands firmly gripping the sides, he began to climb, trying to shield the candle from the myriad of drips. The shaft was a little wider than his shoulders, and he had to be careful not to snag himself on the wet, slippery walls.

He counted the steps—twenty—then thirty, and the water no longer pelted him on the head. He raised the candle and saw the goal—he had reached the second level of the mine. He climbed out of the shaft and found he was at the end of the drift. Toward the entrance, he could make out the glow of daylight coming from outside. Because of the slope of the mountain, he realized the upper level was shorter—and straight.

The ladder was too long to remove from the shaft, so he pulled it up as high as he could, pulled out his hunting knife, and began whittling a deep notch in the frame on both sides. He worked quickly, and once the notches were deep enough, he grabbed the rung just below with one hand, then snapped the frame. He pulled the ladder up again and did the same thing, then let go. The ladder, now twelve feet short of the second level, fell down the shaft. *By the time they find the ladder and backtrack, I'll be long gone.*

The upper level was drier—no fear of water putting out the candle as he proceeded toward the light of the entrance. No rails graced the floor of the drift—Derik wondered if its sole purpose was to provide ventilation to the lower level.

He continued, moving faster as the light from the entrance grew brighter. He reached the opening and stopped short, grabbing for something to hold on to, and finding nothing, fell backward to stop his forward movement—nearly sliding into midair. He cursed silently as he realized the entrance to the upper level was driven into a sheer cliff. A twisted, rusting piece of wire rope several feet long hung from a rusty chunk of iron driven into the wall.

He looked around for a rope to tie to it, but the drift was void of any remnants of equipment or tools. Twelve feet below the entrance was a sloping shelf of rock that obstructed the view of the mine dump below. Beyond that, he could just barely see the roof of the cabin. Climbing down was impossible—once he reached the shelf, there would be no way to prevent sliding to his death. He thought about returning to the ladder, then it dawned on him—he was a prisoner of his own making.

"Devil it!" he said quietly as he turned quickly, bashing his head against the iron sticking from the wall. He fell to the floor of the drift in a heap.

† † †

"This is a dead end," said Jack.

"He's got to be down the main drift—I just hope he didn't double back," said Thomas.

"Sdzeè and John can hold their own," said Jack as they turned and hurried back toward the main drift.

They reached the intersection and stopped. Thomas shined the lamp toward the portal. "What do you think—should we head to the entrance to make sure or press on?"

"Let's move on. If there was any trouble, the gunfire would have echoed like mad inside here."

Thomas nodded and turned down the main drift, holding the revolver in his right hand and the carbide lamp in the left.

"How's the arm holding up," said Jack.

"Stiff and sore, but I'm managing."

"If we run into trouble, let me take the lead."

In the distance, the light from their carbide lamps bounced off the end of the drift. They looked at each other, surprised that Van Sant wasn't there. As they reached the end, the ladder came in view. Thomas shined the lamp upwards but couldn't see the top. "This could be ugly."

"Especially if he's waiting," said Jack. He looked at Thomas—he was standing against the wall, resting his left arm at his side. "I'll go."

"Be careful."

Jack extinguished the carbide lamp and shoved it in his pocket. He gripped the ladder firmly with his left hand and stepped up on the first rung. "Give me some light," he said as he started climbing, keeping the revolver in his right hand pointed upward at the ready.

Thomas pointed the lamp up the shaft but knew Jack would be climbing the last bit in the dark. Jack continued—the light from below grew dimmer with each step. Thomas could no longer see him but kept the light pointed upward.

The rungs were wet and slippery, and holding with one hand proved challenging. Several times he started to slip and wrapped his arm around the side of the ladder the keep from falling. It was nearly pitch black as he took a step up, reached for the next rung, and found it wasn't there. He fell forward, his head smashing against the rock wall above the end of the ladder. He recoiled, his left foot slipping as he dropped the revolver and frantically grabbed for the edge.

Thomas heard the commotion, then the bouncing of the revolver off the walls as it sped downward. He stepped out of the way as it landed next to him, the hammer striking the ground first. The round in the chamber went off, and the slug hit the roof of the adit, showering Thomas with lead and splinters of rock. The noise was excruciating, temporarily deafening him.

Jack came down the ladder, sliding and missing half the rungs on the way down. "You alright?" he yelled.

Thomas nodded. "What happened?"

"The fool cut the ladder off. No way to get up there now."

"Are you sure?"

"I think so," said Jack, just as they became aware of yelling coming from the direction of the entrance.

Fearing the worst, they sprinted toward the portal, Jack lighting his lamp on the run. As they neared the entrance, they could hear Sdzeè.

"Thomas! Jack! Are you alright?"

Their eyes took a moment to adjust as they emerged from the darkness. Sdzeè ran up to Thomas and put her arms around him. "Did you find him?"

"No, but there is an upper level. We think he climbed up there and destroyed the ladder so we couldn't follow."

Sdzeè looked straight up. "I don't see anything except something hanging down from above that overhang."

"I think that's the remnants of a tram line. The miners must have cut it and removed the equipment when they left," said Jack.

"So there is an upper level," said John.

"Yes, and Van Sant made it up to it."

"Now what? Go after him?" said John.

Thomas shook his head. "We can't get up there, and he probably got away. For all we know, there may be another level or exit somewhere."

Jack backed away from the entrance, all the while looking up. He walked down the slope toward the cabin and looked up again. This time he could just see the edge of the adit on the upper level.

"What are you doing?" said John.

"I want to make sure he's not sitting up there ready to take a shot at us."

They moved together as a group until they reached the cabin. Only a portion of the opening on the second level was visible—the lower half hid from view. Sdzeè kept the .45-70 pointed upward as they moved toward the horses. There was no sign of Van Sant.

"I say we get out of here," said Jack. "I'll make sure everyone in town knows about Van Sant. If he shows his face, we'll know about it."

"I, for one, am all for going home," said John as he turned toward the cabin. "I'm ready to kiss my bride and have some of her home cooking."

"I'll go for that—the cooking at least," said Thomas.

"Our horses are stashed down at timberline," said Jack. "John, you and Sdzeè take the two from here. Thomas and I will walk."

"No," said Sdzeè. "I will walk. You have done enough for one day, Thomas Thornton."

Thomas opened his mouth to protest, but she put her finger on his lips and pointed at the horse with her other hand. Thomas smiled and took her by the hand, then kissed her cheek.

"That's enough now—get on that horse," she said. "We can be to Stella's before dark if we hurry."

CHAPTER 24

The lantern hung from a hook above the railing, illuminating the porch of the boarding house. John saw it before the others. *Stella was waiting.*

He kicked the horse into a gallop—Thomas and Sdzeè struggling to keep up. The sound of the horses alerted her, and before they reached the house, Stella leaped down the stairs and was on a dead run toward them.

John reined in the horse and jumped down just as Stella reached him. She nearly knocked him over as she embraced him tightly. "You're home—you're safe."

"I'm fine—a little bruised and battered, so don't squeeze me too hard," said John.

Sdzeè and Thomas caught up. "Thank you for finding him," said Stella.

"It was a group effort, and without Jack, we may not have succeeded," said Thomas.

"Where is Jack? I want to thank him."

"He headed home for some food and much deserved rest—said something about frying up a big batch of chicken and roasting some baked potatoes."

"You should have brought him along. I would have cooked him a feast."

"You'll have time to thank him," said John. "Let's take care of the horses so I can sit down—we'd have

243

been here before dark, but it took longer to get off the mountain than we expected."

"Mountain?" said Stella.

"I'll tell you all about—later," said John.

"I've got the horses," said Thomas. "Go on in—I'll be there in a bit."

"I will help you," said Sdzeè.

They watched as Stella and John walked to the boarding house, arm in arm. "Will he be alright?" said Sdzeè.

"He's tough enough, just needs some rest and food to recover."

Sdzeè nodded as she followed Thomas into the barn. They removed the saddles, then brushed each of the horses down. Thomas favored his wounded arm but managed to fetch a bucket of oats for each horse, something they rarely got. He patted each of them. "They served us well."

"I wonder about Van Sant's horse—do you think he bought it or stole it from someone?" said Sdzeè.

"Knowing him, it could go either way. I didn't see a brand on it anywhere, but that's not unusual for horses up here."

"I would hate for one of us to get shot riding a stolen horse."

"I'll ask around in town—see if anyone has reported one stolen. If not, I guess we gained another horse. Let's go in and see if we can beg something to eat," said Thomas.

Sdzeè laughed. "You know with Stella you have to beg for her to stop feeding you."

† † †

It was late when the trio finished telling Stella all that happened—and how Van Sant was in the wind. At the news, worry spread across her face, but John assured her he wouldn't get the upper hand again—especially not after they spread the word in Valdez and up and down the trail. She felt a little comfort from the thought but still looked concerned.

"The truth is, we don't know where he is," said Thomas. "He could have escaped the mine, or he could still be in there. The latter is my hope."

"The whole thing was pointless," said Stella. "What made him think any of us knew the answer to Preston's vague gibberish."

"I think he was grasping at straws," said John. "He was desperate for money."

"Why didn't Preston just tell him where the money was—in that letter he read to you?" said Stella.

"Because plain and simple, Preston Van Sant was an evil, self-centered, narcissist," said John.

"A ts'olnüüdn," said Sdzeè.

They looked at her quizzically. "Oh. A devil it means."

"You could say that," said Thomas.

"Will we ever figure out where the money went?" said Stella.

Thomas looked at his pocket watch and smiled. "I have some ideas, but it's going to take more brainpower than I can muster tonight. But tomorrow, after one of your fabulous breakfasts, let's work on it."

"I'll have it ready for you at first light," said Stella.

"Can't we wait until a couple hours after that?" said Thomas. "I think none of us wants to get up that early."

Stella smiled and patted his hand. "Whatever you want, Thomas."

† † †

Despite planning to sleep late the next morning, everyone was up well before eight. After breakfast, Stella turned her attention to John, fussing over his bumps and bruises until he jokingly waved her off. She then focused on Thomas' gunshot wound, changing the bandage and announcing it was healing well. Her medical rounds complete, she joined the rest of them at the table, but not before making sure everyone had fresh refills of coffee and attempting to push more eggs, bacon, fried potatoes, and fresh bread on them.

Jack arrived before noon, having spent most of the morning making the rounds to the hotels and shops, warning them to be on the lookout for Van Sant. Stella thanked him profusely for helping in the search and insisted he sit down and have pie and coffee—which he did without protest.

Stella turned to Jack, her face grim. "Do you think we have anything to worry about—I mean with Van Sant returning?"

Jack swallowed the last piece of pie and took a swig of coffee. "Don't think so, but we shouldn't let our guard down for a while. He's going to have a hard time doing anything in town without someone realizing who he is."

"What about the clue to the money?" said Sdzeè. "Does anyone have any ideas?"

Thomas slapped his hand on the table. "We've been so busy I forgot to tell you about something Sdzeè and I heard at the saloon."

"That is right," said Sdzeè.

John leaned in. "What is it."

Thomas explained meeting the blonde Destiny and how she told them she was named after her hometown, Tacoma.

"How does Destiny have anything to do with Tacoma?" said Jack.

John snapped his fingers in the air. "I can't believe I didn't think of that after all the years I spent doing business in Seattle and Tacoma."

"Well, you probably weren't thinking about it being a proper name, even though it was in capital letters," said Thomas.

"So why is it called Destiny?"

"At the time, Northern Pacific was deciding where the terminus of the transcontinental railroad would be, and they chose Tacoma. This brought people, jobs, and the telegraph line to the town, so someone decided it was to be the *City of Destiny*."

"Wait—Northern Pacific?" said Thomas.

"Right, that was...Thomas, do you have the paper from Van Sant's coat handy?"

"It's upstairs—didn't want to keep it on me for obvious reasons. Be back in a jiffy."

"What are you thinking, John?" said Stella.

John smiled. "I think I've figured out most of the puzzle, and it's pretty obvious."

Thomas returned and laid the paper on the table. John slid it over in front of him. "Here, look. We have *Destiny* and then *NP*"

"Your Destiny lies on the NP before you leave," said Stella, reading it aloud.

John nodded. "NP—Northern Pacific. Van Sant was talking about the train."

"So the money is on the train? That makes no sense, especially after all this time," said Jack.

"He could have hidden it somewhere on a train, but you can imagine how many engines and cars have traveled that railway since then. It could be anywhere," said Thomas.

"We must be missing something, but knowing Van Sant and his penchant for being malicious, the whole thing could be a red herring," said John.

"Red herring?" said Sdzeè. "A fish?"

They laughed, and she blushed. "You laugh at me."

Thomas took her hand. "No, it's just funny how you took it. A red herring is a clue that is false—meant to distract from the real truth."

"I see. Do you think it is a...red herring?"

"I don't know," said John. "Let's think about it. If Van Sant really planned for Derik to find the money in the event of his death, it has to all be here on this paper."

"What about this?" said Jack pointing at the word *befour* on the paper. "Why is before spelled that way?"

"I wondered about that," said John. "Van Sant must have spelled it that way for a reason."

"Maybe it's meant to be the number," said Jack. "Why spell it that way, unless he was illiterate."

"Well, he wasn't that. So if it is a number, what does it represent?"

"Be four...be four," said Stella. "B4—a capital *B* and the number four?"

"That might be it," said John excitedly. "Now what does it represent—anyone know? I have an idea."

"What?" said Sdzeè.

"Here's a hint—A1, A2, A3, B1, B2, B3, B4, in a railway station," said John. "Well?"

Thomas and Jack spoke at the same time. "Lockers!"

"Right, they're lockers in a railway station. The money isn't on a train—it's in locker B4 at the *Northern Pacific* terminal in Tacoma," said John.

"Are you sure?" said Stella.

"We won't know until we have a look."

"What are the odds that locker still contains the money after nearly two years?" said Jack.

"It's a long shot but worth a look. Hopefully, Van Sant paid for a long-term rental of the locker."

"Wait—what about the key? Don't you need a key to get into it?" said Stella.

"That is a minor problem, one my man in Seattle can solve for us," said John.

† † †

John sipped the last of his coffee and set the cup on the dining room table. He finished penning the letter, folded it neatly, addressed the envelope, and sealed it. "Ten days at least before we hear something from *Jackson Investigations* in Seattle."

Stella nodded. "It would have been faster to send a telegram, but I understand why you chose a letter."

"It's a sensitive matter, and the way the telegraph shop is run in town, nothing is secret or sacred. We are so close now—I don't want to risk anyone getting in the way."

"Will we have to wait for a letter to find out what happens?"

"I told them to send word by telegraph—but word it carefully."

Stella nodded as Thomas and Sdzeè came in from outside. "Enjoy your afternoon walk?"

"Yes, it is warm today and very nice," said Sdzeè.

"Did you decide if you're leaving?"

Thomas shook his head. "We'd like to stay and see how this plays out, but I'm itching to get back to mining—not making any money here." He smiled and took a seat.

John stood, letter in hand. "It's going to be a while before we hear anything. Seven to ten days for the letter to make it to Seattle, and that's if we get it on a steamer today."

"There's nothing more for you and Sdzeè to do here, Thomas," said Stella.

"What if Van Sant comes back?" said Sdzeè. "Maybe we should stay for a few days longer."

"I think we'll be fine. We left him up that valley without a horse. The walk back to town will give him time to think better of coming after us again," said John.

"And we will be on the lookout just in case," said Stella. "You two should head home and work on getting John's share of gold out of the ground."

Thomas laughed. "You won't need any gold once the money is recovered."

"Can't let you off that easily," said John.

"Alright, alright. Sdzeè and I will get back to work."

† † †

CHAPTER 25

"It will be two weeks tomorrow," said Stella.

John swallowed the last bite of eggs and took a swig of coffee. "I know. They're getting sick of me at the telegraph office."

"I know you're anxious, but going there twice a day isn't helping your stress level any."

John smiled at her. "Thanks for breakfast. I think I'll—"

"Head to the telegraph office?"

"No—I...uh...yes, but I'll only go once today—I promise."

"Maybe you should wait until later in the day."

John stood up and reached for his plate, but Stella snatched it away, along with his cup and fork. "I'll do that."

"Oh, I talked to Jack when I was in town yesterday."

"Which time?"

"Would you stop?"

Stella laughed, then turned serious. "John, you know if we never have that money, it will be fine."

"I know. Part of it's the principle of the thing."

"So, what did Jack have to say."

"No one has seen Van Sant—none of the hotels, the steamship office, or any of the stores."

251

"Does that mean we can stop locking the doors?"

"We need to vigilant, but after this much time, I don't think he'll show his face around here.

I wonder what's become of him?"

"I suppose he could have stowed away on a steamer headed south—I wouldn't put it past him."

"What if he's still up there?"

"Up where—Sulphide Gulch?"

"Yes."

John shook his head, then rubbed his chin. "I suppose it's possible, but if I were a betting man, I'd say he got away. Frankly, I don't care where he is—I'm done with the Van Sants."

"I think I am too. Now get going—you know you want to, but be careful."

John smiled and nodded. "Don't worry, I'll be looking over my shoulder the whole way."

† † †

The telegraph operator finished scribbling down the message, tore it off the pad, and handed it to the clerk. "Thank goodness."

"What?" said the clerk.

"It's a message for Palmer. Now he can stop harassing us."

"Unless it's not what he's looking for."

The operator grunted and went back to copying an incoming message. "Keep that one on top—he'll probably be here any minute."

No sooner had he spoke than the door opened, and John walked in. "Any message—"

"Here it is," said the clerk, thrusting the message forward. "From *Jackson Investigations* in Seattle."

"At last," said John. He took the message and held it at his side.

"Aren't you going to read it? You've been waiting for it."

John shook his head. "Yes, I'm trying to steel myself in case it's bad news."

The clerk looked down and pretended to sort messages. John held the telegram tight. *Can't read this here.* He stashed it in his pocket and left the office. He unhitched the horse, mounted up, and headed slowly down the street, the weight of the message in his pocket increasing with each step. At the edge of town, he stopped, looked around, and read the telegram:

```
JOHN PALMER
VALDEZ ALASKA

JOHN:

TERMINAL WAS REMODELED OVER A
YEAR AGO. ALL LOCKERS WERE
REPLACED. ABANDONED CONTENTS
WERE SOLD AS A LOT AT AUCTION
TEN MONTHS AGO.

YOUR ITEM UNTRACEABLE. PLEASE
ADVISE IF YOU NEED FURTHER
ASSISTANCE.

/S/ CHARLES JACKSON
JACKSON INVESTIGATIONS
SEATTLE WASHINGTON
```

He crumpled the message in his hand and spurred the horse onward.

† † †

They sat on the porch bench—Stella read the message, then handed it back to John.

"So it was all for nothing," said Stella. "Taking you and Thomas hostage—the violence—all for nothing."

John nodded. "What a waste."

"And what of the gold he stole from us?"

"He must have sold it, or it's hidden somewhere," said John. "I don't think he sold it—at least not to the Gold Dust Exchange."

"Did you send word to Thomas? I'm sure they will want to know."

"I didn't, but will. So now we are poor."

Stella took him by the hand, looked up at him, and smiled. "Are we John? Are we?"

They stood together. John put his arms around her and hugged her tightly. He looked across the valley, beyond the Lowe River—to Sulphide Gulch.

EPILOGUE

The raven soared in circles above the valley, finally locking its wings, the bright sunlight glistening off the jet black feathers. It glided downward, making a perfect landing on the rusting iron protruding from the entrance. It sat there, bobbing its head up and down. Stepping sideways along the iron, it reached the end, then hopped down to the floor of the adit just a few feet inside.

The raven strutted forward cautiously, unsure if what lay ahead would lash out. The emaciated body remained motionless. The crumpled letter pinned underneath the body flapped in the gentle breeze. The raven cocked its head, attracted by the shiny object clutched in the bony fingers. It pecked at it, grabbed it in its beak, and repeatedly pulled until it came free and dropped to the rocky floor.

A key was attached to the shiny metal fob and engraved on it, a capital *B* and the number four. The raven picked up the fob, hopped to the entrance, and lunged forward, spreading its wings. It circled once over the cabin, then turned, gliding down the valley toward the Lowe River.

> "I have seen all the works that are done under the sun; and indeed, all is vanity and grasping for the wind." —*Ecclesiastes 1:14*

THE END

GLOSSARY OF TERMS

This is a glossary of mining and other terms used in the book. For some terms there may be more than one definition, but the one provided here is in the historical context of the story.

adit: *A horizontal mine working, usually driven into the side of a hill*

ch'inee'iin: Thief

drift: *A horizontal underground working in a mine.*

dump: See *winter dump*

paydirt: *Gold bearing gravels*

placer: *A gold deposit found in recent or ancient stream gravels*

portal: *The entrance to a horizontal mine working*

shnuudeh: *Sweetheart*

sluice box: *A wooden box with riffles used to process gravel and capture gold.*

sluicing: *Running gravel through a sluice box to recover gold*

shaft: *A vertical mine working that provides underground access, usually timbered for support.*

timber set: *Timbers erected around a mine opening or within an underground mine to prevent a cave in*

ts'olnüüdn: *Devil*

udzih: *Caribou*

winter dump: *Material excavated from an underground drift mine during the winter and stockpiled for sluicing during the summer.*

About the Author

G.E. Sherman has a wide and varied background, including that of geologist, mining engineer, software engineer, and author. He has authored both technical books and articles, as well as fiction. In addition to being the founder of the popular open source QGIS project, he has published several books on the topic.

When writing fiction, he draws on the depth of his background, providing vivid descriptions of life on the last frontier, wildlife encounters, and survival. Further, his experience as an outdoor enthusiast provides inspiration in the stories he tells.

G.E. Sherman resides in Alaska and regularly watches moose from his living room window.